7112127

Juv
B

Bishop, Curtis

Little League
visitor

WITHDRAWN

Please do not remove the date
due slip from this pocket.

WASHINGTON COUNTY
LIBRARY SYSTEM

LITTLE LEAGUE VISITOR

LITTLE LEAGUE VISITOR

O

Curtis Bishop

J. B. LIPPINCOTT COMPANY

PHILADELPHIA

NEW YORK

7112127

Copyright © 1966 by Curtis Bishop
Printed in the United States of America
Library of Congress Catalog Card Number: 66–10894
Fourth Printing

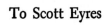

To Scott Eyres

Contents

CHAPTER 1

O

The New Boy Can Chunk

"We'll just get started," grumbled Dick Merrill, "and then we will have to rehearse. I wish we had never gotten ourselves into this mess."

"We can practice until he gets here," Keith Gregg insisted, leading the way into the roomy Gregg back yard. He had a ball, his worn catcher's mitt for Dick, a new first baseman's pad for himself, and a bat repaired from last year's damage. A small split had ruled out the latter for official league play but several small nails and adhesive tape made it solid enough for pepper games in a back yard.

Keith stood an inch taller than Dick but no heavier. Dick, at eleven, a year younger, was built like a catcher, stocky and strong. So was Keith and he had caught regularly the previous season. But a cut artery during the winter ruled out backstopping for him this season. He could throw underhanded or sidearmed but not "from off his ear." He meant to win some other starting position though, either at first base or in the outfield.

Hence, the first baseman's mitt which he had not used yet and was anxious to try out.

His injury, unless the Giants acquired a new receiver in the player auction, left the year's catching responsibility to Dick. He would do all right, too, believed Keith, with experience and improved pegging. Dick had relieved Keith behind the plate more than once in the previous season.

"You get Dick ready to catch," Manager Jim Tracy had told Keith the previous day, "and we can spend all our points for a pitcher."

Keith had promised. Dick had showed a disposition the previous season to take practice too casually. This year he had to rise and shine, and Keith had been telling him so.

The two boys swapped easy tosses a few minutes, then Keith ordered his friend to throw harder. "Fire the ball," he said. "You won't build up your arm this way."

"No use getting hot and sweaty," Dick argued. "We have that silly old rehearsal at four-thirty."

"Your mother got us into it," Keith answered, sighing at Dick's lack of enthusiasm. Manager Tracy would correct that when official practice started, of course; no boy took it easy for him, especially not his catcher. But Keith wanted the coach satisfied with Dick's improvement before the tryouts and the auction.

"Harder," Keith said again. He had a problem of his own to solve, use of the first baseman's mitt. He must learn to catch the ball between thumb and forefinger, not easy after two years of shifting his weight so as to take a pitch in the deep pocket of a catcher's pad.

The day before he had stepped off twenty paces, the approximate distance between home plate and first base.

The Gregg yard was not large enough for the most vital throw to practice—from home to second for Dick, from first to third for Keith. But Mrs. Gregg had ruled against play in the street and the scheduled rehearsal allowed no time for practice at Westenfield playground.

"You worry about this Boy Scout show until Thursday night," Mrs. Gregg had ordered. "Then you can go as wild about baseball as you like."

The professional singer with whom the "Unholy Three" were to perform was not due for rehearsal until four-thirty; the two boys had that long to limber up their throwing arms. The sidearmed motion was awkward for Keith still, even after hours of slamming a tennis ball against the garage wall. It was enough to bring tears to his eyes again. Here he had been sure of repeating as an all-star team catcher and perhaps dividing time with some new twelve-year-old Giant on the pitcher's mound and it was all he could do to throw with reasonable accuracy from twenty paces! The arm which all West Austin Little League opponents had learned to respect might never be the same, though the family doctor said not to give up hope. Persistent effort and determination, he said, often accomplished what medical skill could not.

"What's keeping Luke?" asked Dick.

Luther Doyle was the third member of the Den 22 musical ensemble. In baseball he played infield for the Calumet Cats and had also earned all-star honors as an eleven-year-old.

"He won't be here 'til four-thirty," Keith said without thinking.

Dick stopped in the act of throwing. "You told me four o'clock."

So Keith had—to provide this short practice period before their rehearsal with Sonny Barton.

Sonny Barton! Keith grunted in disgust as he gestured for Dick to resume throwing. That had been some idea of Dick's mother—to invite the recording star to sing at the Scout minstrel with the den's own trio providing background. To the surprise of everyone but Mrs. Merrill, the rock and roll singer had accepted. Keith had heard the bad news with his own ears as Mrs. Merrill had exulted to his mother.

"He was the nicest thing about it," Dick's mother had gurgled. "You know how he talks, with that exaggerated southern accent. 'Ah like to help out kids,' he told me. 'Ah will be glad to oblige, ma'am.' "

Keith sighed at the recollection. Mothers sometimes did not seem to care what they got their boys into. The den needed the money, sure, but this was proving no small ordeal for him, Dick, and Luke. The forthcoming novelty show was the talk of O. Henry Junior High School, with two entirely different sets of reactions. The boys teased the three young victims unmercifully. *So you are going to sing with Sonny Barton! Now isn't that just ducky! Are you going to deck out in duds like his—tight black trousers and yellow shirt and black hat with bells around the brim!*

The girls thought it "just wonderful," of course, which added to the strain. Who wanted to be the center of such female attention? Barbee Brush, who lived next door, thought it the grandest thing ever to be scheduled for West Austin. She just "couldn't wait" to see Sonny drive up in front of the Gregg house and to "see him in person, even if it's just across the fence." She was sixteen now, four years older than Keith.

He heard the doorbell, a faint sound in the back yard, and grunted again.

"That's Luke now," Dick guessed.

Keith hoped so, for he wanted this Sonny Barton to arrive late and leave as soon as possible. He had said he could only spare a few minutes, according to Mrs. Merrill. Well, the fewer the better.

"If it's Luke, he can come on out," Keith said. "We can have a pepper game until this dude singer gets here."

But it was not Luke Doyle. Instead Mrs. Gregg ushered a wiry black-haired boy of about their own age into the back yard.

"Boys, we have a visitor," she said sweetly. "I want you to meet Tom Barton, Sonny's younger brother. Tom, this is Dick Merrill and my own Keith."

Keith sighed. What a way to introduce him—"my own Keith"! When would his mother realize that he was no longer a baby?

"Tom is here to meet his brother," Mrs. Gregg explained. "Now suppose you two put away that baseball and entertain your company."

"Please don't," the visitor said quickly. "I would like to join in their catch game, if I may."

Keith looked at the visitor with new respect. There was a close resemblance to Sonny Barton's photographs, all right —dark features and eyes, jet black hair and sort of delicate good looks. Keith's eyes gleamed, and he wished he could fire the ball with last year's speed. It would be funny to watch this boy try to catch a really hard throw.

"I should have known it," said Mrs. Gregg with a smile. "All boys your age seem to be wild about baseball. Well, pitch right in with them, Tom. I will call you when your brother arrives."

Now Dick sensed Keith's thoughts and showed a mischievous grin, too. This Tom Barton did not dress as outlandishly as his famous brother, but his clothes were flashier and more expensive than those worn by the usual boy of such age. Tom shed a light camel's-hair sweater and stood in white silk sports shirt and regular slacks in contrast to the T-shirts and blue jeans worn by Keith and Dick.

"I'll get you a glove," Keith offered. "It may be a little small for you—I haven't used it much in the last two years. I've been catching."

"Thank you," the handsome boy said politely.

For once Keith found something without his mother's assistance. The worn glove was in his bottom dresser drawer. It was in good condition still, adequate enough for a boy nine or ten years old. But this singer's brother—he must be thirteen anyhow, maybe older. Keith chuckled. If he could just get Dick to fire the ball at their visitor now!

"It's the best I can dig up," he apologized to Tom Barton.

The unexpected visitor nodded. "It'll do," he said, "though I'm used to a bigger glove. I have big hands for my size."

So he did, realized Keith. And a term often used by Manager Tracy flashed through his mind—"good hands."

"We'll take turns throwing to Dick," Keith explained.

"I'm trying to make a catcher out of him. He has to take my place this year on our little league team."

"Why? Are you too old for another season?"

"No, but I caught my arm and—" Keith threw side-armed and low to Dick. "That's the only way I can throw until a nerve or something comes back to life," he explained. "I'll have to learn to play first base or the outfield or sit on the bench."

"Or second base," Tom Barton said casually. "There any kind of a quick throw is good enough."

Keith was taken aback by the knowing comment. Dick threw to their visitor and threw hard. The visitor took the ball in his undersized glove but could not hold it.

"Not much of a pocket," he said.

No smile came to Keith's face. This Tom Barton had not caught the ball but he had reached for it with a graceful gesture which left no doubt of his training.

He tossed casually to Dick, throwing with an easy three-quarters motion.

"You've played ball before," grunted Keith.

Tom flashed a grin. "Every chance I get."

Another exchange of tosses; this time the visitor threw harder. Keith, taught to study pitchers, both on his own team and the opposition, recognized ability at once.

"Did you play in a regular league?" he asked.

"One year only. Nashville."

Keith hesitated. "Tennessee?"

"Yes," Tom said lightly. This time he caught Dick's return throw easily despite the small glove. He gestured for Dick to provide a lower target, further convincing Keith of previous mound experience. How did Mr. Tracy express it? You could recognize by the way he stood on the mound.

"Why just one year?" Keith asked, now all curiosity, no longer thinking about having sport with this unannounced company.

"My brother was with the Grand Old Opery all last summer," Tom said, "so I was eligible for a league there. The other summers—well, he travels around a lot."

Keith nodded. A singer would, of course, especially one as well-known as Sonny Barton.

"You go with him all the time?"

"No, just between school semesters."

Another graceful delivery. He threw harder each time, observed Keith.

"But school isn't out yet," he said. This was early April; the school year at O. Henry would not end until May 31.

"Oh, I don't go to public schools," Tom explained. "I wish I could, but it wouldn't work—not the way we live. The academy I go to—it's in Tennessee—has a three-term schedule. Our semester ended last Monday and I flew here to meet my brother."

Another easy catch, a still faster pitch to Dick. "I will stay with him for six weeks," added the olive-skinned boy, "and then go back to Dexter Academy. There is no reason for me to stay in school the year round. Sonny doesn't want me to rush through. I will be ready for college when I'm seventeen and he thinks that is early enough."

Keith frowned. "Does your brother—is he your guardian—or——?"

His voice fell off. He did not know how to express the question he wanted to ask.

"Not legally," Tom said evenly, as if explanation did not come hard at all. "We have no parents, you see. They were drowned in a flood when I was a baby. Sonny supports me, but I am a ward of a Tennessee district court until he is twenty-one." A smile touched his handsome features. "But the judge there leaves most of it up to Sonny. He takes good care of me."

"How old are you anyhow?"

"Almost thirteen."

"When is your birthday?"

"August 3."

"Gosh," Keith exclaimed, "then you are eligible for another year of Little League."

"Sure."

Now Tom held up two fingers as a warning to Dick. And the curve ball he threw broke low and into the dirt, getting away from the would-be catcher. Keith sighed. When would Dick learn to shift his weight instead of trying to stab at the ball!

"I wish I could play this season," Tom said wistfully as Dick retrieved the ball. "We were counting on a championship team at Nashville this year. My league all-star team reached the state finals last season."

How well did Tennessee all-star teams perform? Keith hesitated, then put the question.

"The team that beat us went to Williamsport," shrugged Tom. "It was Chattanooga."

Keith took a deep breath. The West Austin All-Stars had been eliminated in the district tournament. And the Texas champions, from Fort Worth, had gotten nowhere in intra-state competition.

"Were you on the all-star team?"

"Yes. I pitched some, in relief." The visitor sighed. "I gave up the home run which beat us," he said ruefully.

Dick's throw came to Keith. He caught it, held the ball an instant to look directly at the singer's brother.

"Is there any chance of you playing in West Austin this year?" he demanded. "We need a pitcher the worst way. We don't have anybody back. And our manager—he is Mr. Jim Tracy—has bonus points from last season. If a good pitching prospect tries out, we can buy him—if Mr. Tracy wants him."

"I doubt it," Tom said with a sigh. "Sonny and I have talked about it. He wants me to play somewhere. But being eligible—"

"You just have to live in the league area," Keith pointed out.

"Sure," Tom said, throwing again, "but that—"

Dick's complaint interrupted him. "You got a sponge?" the catcher demanded of Keith. "I don't want a sore hand before practice even starts. And this guy is firing."

"I am sorry," apologized Tom. "I will ease up."

Keith sighed again. He could not remember Dick complaining of a pitcher's speed before, not even last season when he had caught Merle Conroy.

"Why couldn't you live in West Austin for this season, you and your brother?" he demanded. Tom Barton, he had decided, could well be the solution to the dilemma of the Atlas Giants.

"We just couldn't," Tom said at once. "Sonny has his career to consider."

"There is no chance at all?" Keith persisted. He found

himself liking this wiry dark-haired boy, even after his instant prejudice against him.

"That's up to Sonny," shrugged Tom. "He has a manager and an agent but he makes most decisions for himself. And he does want me to play baseball."

"You should," Keith declared. "If you can do other things as well as you throw——"

"Better, I think," Tom said without the slightest show of braggadocio. "Sonny knows baseball. He wants me to learn to be an all-around player, then let my college coach decide whether I should pitch or play somewhere else."

"Gosh, I'd have never thought about your brother being——"

Keith felt like biting off his own tongue. But Tom Barton was not offended. "I know what you mean," he said with another of those broad smiles. "I have read some of these things about my brother. But remember he is in show business and he has to get publicity and put on a front. I'll bet you end up liking him."

Keith held back his thoughts. He doubted that very much. Anybody who dressed and acted like Sonny Barton!

But if there was a chance, even a slim one, that the singer's brother could play in West Austin——!

Just then Luke Doyle came through the gate, guitar under his arm. He took in the situation at a glance. "Why didn't you tell me to bring my glove?" he demanded of Keith.

Luke was short and freckle-faced and as eager a little leaguer as his fellow members of the Den 22 guitar group. He shared Keith's opinion of the forthcoming show, too. Mrs. Merrill, he had fumed when told about it, was a busybody for planning it and especially for wangling Sonny Barton into a benefit appearance.

"We are just quitting," Keith said, collecting the two mitts and worn gloves. "We had better go in and wait for Mr. Barton."

"Don't call him that," smiled the singer's brother. "He is Sonny everywhere he goes, and to everybody."

"What are we quitting for?" demanded Dick. "He isn't here yet. One minute you are riding me to practice every chance we get and the next——"

"We have to get this fool show out of the way," Keith shrugged, flashing his teammate a warning glance.

He had not introduced Tom to the third musical light of Den 22. Tom took that upon himself.

"I'm Tom Barton, Sonny's brother," he said politely to Luke.

"I'm Luke Doyle," was the unhappy answer, "and I've been roped into this deal, too."

"Is it so bad?" Tom asked with a faint smile.

"It's terrible," Luke said unhesitantly. "We may never live it down."

"You mean—appearing with Sonny Barton?" The younger brother was amused and did not bother to conceal it.

"Sure," Luke said tersely.

Tom's smile broadened. "I suppose he doesn't appeal to your age level. But that is on purpose. It's the teen-age crowd who buy records, not little league players."

"That's for sure," declared Luke. "My sister is nuts about him—that's how this business got started. We started out—well, to make her mad—she gets fired up at the way we sort of make fun——"

He realized he had said too much and his freckled features went even redder with embarrassment.

Tom's dark eyes flashed. "Your act is a takeoff on my brother?"

Keith realized it was time to intervene. "Well, sort of," he said weakly. "You see, we aren't much on singing. Playing either. But we just got to fooling around on rainy days and——"

"Does my brother know this?"

"Gosh, we don't know," Keith said unhappily. "We don't know what Mrs. Merrill said to him."

Tom's lips went tight. "Then I hope he refuses to go through with it," he snapped. "He is a famous singer in spite of whether you like him or not. He consented to this benefit in good faith, to help your scout den raise money for your summer camp. You couldn't pack enough people into your scout hall to pay Sonny Barton what he usually gets for one appearance."

"Gosh, Tom, we didn't do it," Keith appealed.

"No use of us trying to hash that out," protested Dick. "Let's have a pepper game until he gets here."

"No," Keith said firmly. "Let's go inside and wait for him." He was feeling a little weak inside, wishing that his two friends could keep their mouths shut. Both seemed to be trying their best to spoil the idea he had just hatched. Luke had hurt the visitor's feelings and Keith was anxious to have Tom's friendship. And what was wrong with his thickheaded teammate, Dick Merrill? Did he want Luke Doyle to find out about Tom Barton's surprising baseball ability? If there was any sort of chance that Tom could play in the West Austin League this year—and Keith had made up his mind to grab at that straw—then it should be kept as quiet as possible. Let Luke find out what Keith had in mind, and how Tom could pitch, and the Calumet infield would hurry the word to his manager, Sneaker Kane. And Keith wanted Jim Tracy of the Giants to be the only West Austin manager with any advance information about Tom Barton, who had played last year in Nashville, Tennessee!

CHAPTER 2

O

Presenting Sonny Barton!

Keith's mother welcomed them inside. "Mr. Barton just called and is on his way," she said a bit excitedly—to her son's disgust. "You boys tune up your instruments and be ready for him. I will fix you lemonade and cookies."

"Let me help you, Mrs. Gregg," Tom offered politely. But his expression plainly showed that he was not completely over his resentment.

"Why, thank you, Tom. But couldn't you help the boys with their instruments? None of them are exceptional musicians, I'm afraid."

"I would be of no assistance at all," he said a bit stiffly. "My brother has never let me touch a guitar."

"I wish I never had," grumbled Luke.

"I am disgusted with all three of you," Mrs. Gregg scolded them. "This will be an experience you can cherish the rest of your lives. I know this; I am proud of the opportunity to welcome him into my home."

"Maybe you like his singing," said Luke.

"As it happens, I am not a fan of his," said Mrs. Gregg with a snap in her voice. "But he is still a celebrity and it is very generous of him to donate his talent. Do you realize that we have sold every single ticket and that you unappreciative boys will enjoy the best camp of your experience because of him?"

Bless his mother's heart, Keith whispered to himself. For the change in Tom's expression was plain to see. Mrs. Gregg had more than undone all of Luke's unflattering words.

"My brother does things like that all over the country," Tom said proudly. "The little league I played in last year—in Nashville, ma'am—it was running into financial troubles —we needed new uniforms and the clubhouse had burned during the winter—and my brother put on a free show that——"

"More than paid off the deficit," nodded Mrs. Gregg. "I am sure of that. We could have sold a thousand tickets to our benefit if the hall were bigger. So you three boy scouts act up to your scout dignity and spirit."

She disappeared into the kitchen. Keith noticed that Luke was staring at their visitor.

"You played little league in Nashville last year?" the Calumet infielder asked slowly.

"Yes," Tom said curtly, "and we got closer to Williamsport than any Texas team."

Keith sighed. Now the cat was out of the bag. He knew that Luke was not about to be satisfied with so little information.

But any further questions were prevented by the appearance of a spectacular convertible outside. Luke saw it first. "Look," he exclaimed, pointing through the picture window of the Gregg living room.

The long yellow automobile slowed down before the Gregg house, passed it slowly, then backed up to a stop. Keith and Dick stared as wide-eyed as Luke.

"Jeepers," muttered Dick, "that's a real showboat."

Keith nodded. Never had he seen such a car.

"Sonny had it built to his own orders," Tom said in that same tight voice. "There is no other model like it."

The three West Austin boys moved to the window as one. Out of the car stepped a youth whose resemblance to Tom Barton showed even at that distance. This was Sonny Barton in person, and no doubt of it. Keith's lips went tight. He must not betray what he was thinking, not with Tom watching him so closely. But what a costume! Gleaming yellow shirt, tight-fitting brown velveteen trousers, black hat decorated with tiny silver bells! Now he took a guitar case out of his car, a gold-plated case no less, and came slowly toward the Gregg door. Besides everything else, Keith thought, this Sonny Barton badly needed a haircut. And those long sideburns—was he trying to hide his face!

Mrs. Gregg came hurrying out of the kitchen and met the singer at the door.

"Come right in, Mr. Barton," she said warmly, extending her hand. "The boys are ready. I am mixing them lemonade."

The singer was not a full grown man, neither in years nor stature. Keith guessed that Sonny Barton weighed no more than a hundred and thirty pounds. And he looked exactly like his pictures.

Sonny smiled at his brother. "So you found the place all right?"

"I found it," Tom said rather shortly. He still wasn't in a good humor, grieved Keith.

"Ah hope my brother hasn't been any trouble," the celebrity apologized to Mrs. Gregg. "Ah had to tape two television shows or else ah wouldn't have had him meet me here."

Keith shut his eyes tightly. That exaggerated drawl added to his garb!

"He has been anything but trouble," Mrs. Gregg said at once. "Keith and Dick were playing ball when he came— they always are—and Tom——"

"Ah reckon he was right at home," the singer grinned. He looked askant at his brother. "You didn't throw too hard, did you? Ah don't know what we can do about your ball playing this year but ah sure don't want you showing up with a sore arm."

"I just bore down on two or three pitches," Tom said. "And just tried two curves."

Keith tried to conceal his reaction to that, his mixed reaction. In the first place, if that was true, then Tom Barton was even better than Keith had realized. Tom had thrown several pitches to Dick which would have baffled any hitter in the West Austin League. And, Keith groaned inwardly, Luke Doyle was now fully curious. His suspicious eyes went from Keith to Dick and back again. That was bad, but the singer's words made up for that. "Ah don't know what we can do about your ball playing this year!"

Then Sonny Barton was willing for his younger brother to enjoy another little league season! If that could be worked out for West Austin, then who cared what Luke Doyle told his manager? Mr. Tracy had extra points; he could outbid any rival coach.

"Now meet your budding successors," Mrs. Gregg said. "This is my son, Keith—and Dick Merrill—his mother made the arrangements with you—and Luther Doyle. I am biased in their favor, of course, but even I cannot claim that they are dedicated musicians, especially not in the spring. They are more interested in baseball now than in music."

"Ah know," Sonny said pleasantly. "Ah have a brother."

"Then you understand. I'm sure you would like to get down to business immediately."

"Yes, ma'am. I have a passel of things——"

"Of course, " Mrs. Gregg said. "Boys, let Mr. Barton have your act."

"Sonny, ma'am. Nobody ever calls me Mr. Barton."

Keith licked his lips, wishing a deep hole could swallow them up temporarily. The routine they had worked out— well, it was as Luke had hinted, and Tom had quickly resented the idea.

"Maybe," Keith said weakly, appealing to his two partners, "we had better try something else instead of 'Teen-Age Queen.' "

"What else do we know?" demanded Luke.

"Well, we messed around some—we tried a couple of numbers straight."

The unabashed Luke shook his head. "I don't want to

try any straight number," he declared. "None of us can sing a lick and if this isn't funny, then—"

Dick, observed Keith, was embarrassed, too. And he was conscious that Sonny Barton's dark eyes were studying each of them in turn.

"Your boys have a novelty number worked up?" the singer asked pleasantly.

"Yes, sir, sort of," Keith said, struggling for words. He licked his dry lips. "You see, Mr. Barton, it's like this——"

"Sonny."

"Yes, sir, Sonny. Well, Luke has a sister who is fifteen and——"

"Sixteen," grunted the freckle-faced boy. "She had a birthday last week."

"Well, sixteen," nodded the desperate Keith. "She is a big fan of yours—has a stack of your records——"

"Good," smiled the singer. "That is my bread and butter. Tom's, too."

Tom came to Keith's rescue. "What Keith is trying to tell you, Sonny," he said grimly, "is that they have a routine making fun of you. I haven't seen it, but I realized that from their talk about it. They worked it up just to aggravate Luke's sister."

Keith ducked his head guiltily. He looked up at his mother's words and again appreciated her quick assistance.

"I did not realize that, Sonny," she said earnestly. "I haven't heard their number myself. It was Mrs. Merrill——"

"Gosh," put in Dick, "my mother didn't know what it was about. She just had this brainstorm and contacted you and——"

"Ah see," nodded the celebrity. Keith could not be sure of Sonny's feelings.

"We didn't want to do it," Luke said. "We still don't. But Mrs. Merrill——"

"She is chairman of the fund-raising committee," Mrs. Gregg said sternly. "I am sure her intentions were the best, Sonny. But if you are——"

"The main thing, ma'am, is to send these boys to camp," the singer said. He turned to the reluctant trio. "Let's hear what you got."

Keith sighed and plucked out the vamp. Luke and Dick joined in with the former's version of the lyrics. They were funny, really, except that now they must be sung confronting the target of their ridicule. They were twelve-year-old boys dreading their 'teens because then they were supposed to become interested in girls and would have to put up with their silly crushes on singers such as Sonny Barton. Their pantomimes were all inspired by Sonny's own contortions and grimaces when singing a love song. Dick, who could actually carry a tune in falsetto, imitated the squealing girls.

They finished. Keith looked hopefully once at their famous visitor, then stared at the floor. Sonny was frowning and there was no humorous glint in his dark eyes.

"Ah will have to think about this," he said. "When is this show?"

"Tomorrow night."

"Ah don't know," he said gravely. "Ah just don't know."

"Gosh, Mr. Barton, forget about it," appealed Keith. "It's a crumby act to start with and asking you to be in it——"

"Ah haven't said ah wouldn't," Sonny said brusquely.

"Ah said ah wanted to think about it. Can you boys be back here tomorrow afternoon for another rehearsal?"

"I have tumbling class," objected Luke.

The singer's eyes flashed again. "If ah can find time for it, so can you," he declared. "Ah will be here at four-thirty."

Keith licked his lips again. "Can Tom—meet you here again?" he asked hopefully. "Can he come early and practice with us some more?"

"I had planned to go to a movie," Tom said.

A movie in preference to baseball! Keith sighed. Tom was being plain enough with his rebuff.

Sonny's eyes studied his brother an instant, then moved to Keith.

"Maybe ah will bring him with me," the singer said lightly. He picked up his guitar case. "Ah have to hustle along now. Ah will see you here tomorrow."

"I hope you will come back, both of you," Mrs. Gregg said earnestly. "It was a pleasure to have Tom in our home even for such a short time."

"Thank you, ma'am," Sonny said politely. "Ah'm sure he enjoyed it, too. He doesn't get much chance to mix with kids his own age when he is traveling around with me. Ah don't really know why he wants to do it."

"I get along all right," Tom said brusquely. He turned to Keith. "So long. Enjoyed the catch game."

And off they went in the specially built convertible. Luke and Dick left soon afterward; their young host had no stomach for any further play. He felt like crying instead. Small chance now of persuading Sonny Barton to let his brother play baseball in the West Austin League this summer! That danged silly song of theirs—it was all Luke's fault. If he hadn't wanted to annoy his sister——

"You must share the blame with Luther," declared his mother when he voiced his feelings. "Mrs. Merrill and I are equally responsible, too. We had no idea your prize routine was a ridicule of Sonny."

"We tried to tell Mrs. Merrill," protested Keith. "We never liked the idea from the start."

"I know," Mrs. Gregg conceded wearily. "But she thought, and so did I, that it was a natural objection against appearing in public." She sighed. "Now we have sold all those tickets," she worried, "and have already spent all of the den's treasury preparing for the show. Otherwise I would insist that she cancel the performance."

"You're in a mess if he won't show up," Keith pointed out.

"We certainly are. But I think he will."

"He didn't say he would."

"He set a second rehearsal." Her lips twitched. "I am ashamed of my part in this. He will go through with it, all right. He is a great performer regardless of how you and I feel about him. He could not afford the adverse publicity, walking out on a scout benefit."

"But he sure isn't going to be happy about it," brooded Keith. "And there goes our chance of getting Tom to play in the league this year."

"In the West Austin League? What made you even think of that?"

"Because he wants to play and Sonny wants him to. He played in Nashville last year and made the all-star team and——"

"Is he really that good?"

"Mother, he would be the best pitcher in the league if we could talk his brother into letting him play here," Keith said firmly. "And we could get him for the Giants, too. Mr. Tracy has more points this year than the other managers."

A smile touched her face. "Now I understand your concern," she said. "Well, I regret it very much. I am almost as interested in the Giants acquiring a pitcher as you are. I enjoyed having my son catch for the league champions last year."

"Yes, ma'am," nodded Keith. She sure had. His mother had not missed a single game. His father either. And, thinking of his father——

"You think maybe Dad can go see Sonny and——?"

Mrs. Gregg sighed. "I am afraid your father is more of a lawyer than he is a diplomat. He is also as prejudiced against Sonny Barton as you and your two friends."

"I've changed my mind," Keith objected. "I'll bet Dick has, too."

"Sure, now that you know his young brother is a pitcher who might help the Giants win again. Let's face it, son. We have messed up any chance of that."

"Yes, ma'am," surrendered Keith. It was easy to believe that they had. Sonny had showed no outward resentment but Tom—it was not likely that Tom would want to play in West Austin even if his brother could make the arrangements. It had been a good idea, but he might as well forget it and look elsewhere for the mound ace the Giants needed this season. Luke and his wild ideas—Mrs. Merrill and her wild schemes for raising money!

"Maybe if you called him at his hotel and asked him and Tom to eat with us tomorrow night——"

"I doubt that would appeal to Sonny Barton. He is used to swank hotels and the best restaurants." She hesitated, then nodded. "But it wouldn't hurt to make the gesture anyhow." She smiled. "I am not getting involved in your recruiting schemes; Jim Tracy is quite competent to pick his own players. But I have unwittingly hurt the feelings of a nice boy. Two boys, in fact—Sonny is just seventeen himself."

"And making all that money?"

"All that money," nodded Mrs. Gregg. "A headliner since he was fifteen. He is really a nice person considering that."

Keith said nothing. He did not have to agree. But he did like Tom. And how that boy could chunk!

CHAPTER 3

O

Sonny Steals a Show

"He accepted," Mrs. Gregg announced as Keith came in the door. "Tom, too. And he asks for nothing special, just a regular family meal."

"You mean—they will really eat with us?"

"Yes. He was very polite about it. He insisted that we shouldn't feel under obligation to him just because he was doing a benefit show. But I could tell by his tone—he and Tom really appreciate the invitation."

Keith beamed. "Then Tom isn't unhappy with us either."

"I didn't talk to him. You call Luke and Dick now and make sure they are on time." She sighed in relief. "I certainly hope the audience is polite tonight. Mrs. Merrill is upset, as I knew she would be."

"If she had just listened to Dick and me——"

"I know, but she was excited over the prospect of solving our money problems. You give Luke a special lecture. Make him see that Sonny is the injured party, not you three scouts."

"I'll try," Keith promised.

"And get right on the telephone. They will be here promptly. Sonny wants to change the routine some."

"I guess take out all the pantomime and——"

"I don't know. But whatever he wants, you boys must do it."

Luke and Dick arrived before the appointed time. Exactly at 4:29 the same yellow vehicle pulled up in the Gregg driveway. In came Sonny, guitar case in hand, with Tom close behind. The latter tried to match his brother's good humor, but Keith sensed that Tom was still far from happy.

"Ah want to spice up the routine," Sonny said, businesslike from almost the moment he entered the house. "You cats have a pretty good idea but you aren't hamming it enough. Ah figger Tom here can lead the pantomime business. He can mock me to a fare-you-well."

"Just in our hotel room," muttered the young brother. "Not on a stage."

"No more of that talk," ordered the singer. He took out his guitar. "Ah will run through my regular routine. You boys take your cues from Tom."

"Oh, all right," the latter muttered.

Sonny went into his act with the "Unholy Three" performing behind him, led by Tom. There was no doubting the younger boy's ability to imitate his brother. Even Luke could not help laughing. Mrs. Gregg tried to control her reactions but found that impossible.

"Tom, you are a born clown," she declared when the

number was concluded. She had laughed so hard that her eyes were filled with tears. "And I am proud of you, Sonny. It takes a big performer to encourage such mimicking."

"If we are gonna have the act, ma'am," he said quietly, "we want it to be a good one. Now let's go through it again, cats. And really clown it up this time. Keep up with Tom."

Luke, Keith, and Dick obeyed. "Is that better?" Sonny asked after this second effort.

"I think it is wonderful," she said. "But I am still worried about the whole thing. I don't believe we should invite you just to make fun of you——"

"Ah have my own ideas about that, ma'am," Sonny said calmly. His dark eyes gleamed. "Ah run into negative audiences before."

"I'm sure you have, but——"

The doorbell interrupted her. Keith opened it to reveal Barbee Brush. He grunted. She had really decked herself out for this quick visit next door. Her hair was all brushed up and she had changed her usual cotton socks for nylons. Her lips trembled but she did not flinch.

"I heard him singing," she told Mrs. Gregg, "and I just couldn't help it. I had to come over for an autograph."

She had a new record album under her arm. Keith's mother looked questioningly at Sonny. He had risen at Barbee's entrance.

"Would you, Sonny?" Mrs. Gregg asked gently. "This is Barbee Brush, our next-door neighbor. She and Keith have played together all their lives."

Not in two or three years, he said to himself, not since she had started doing up her hair and dressing like the other high school girls.

"Ah sure will," Sonny said at once. He took the album and Barbee's ballpoint pen. He scrawled something and handed the record back with a professional smile.

"Oh, thank you," gasped Barbee. "That's just wonderful." She bit her lips. "I have three girl friends at my house," she went on. "They bought albums, too. Would you—could they——?"

Luke had wandered to the window. "Three girls, shucks," he said disgustedly. "There is a whole mob over there."

"Well," apologized Barbee, "the word is spreading around—and everyone recognizes your car——"

"Barbee," protested Mrs. Gregg, "Sonny and his brother are our guests and——"

"Ah don't mind," the singer interrupted. "When they don't pay any attention, that's when ah will worry." He took Barbee's elbow. "But let's don't bring them all in here," he suggested. "Ah will come over to your house and ah will autograph all the albums you and your friends have."

"You don't have to, Sonny," Mrs. Gregg said quickly.

He smiled at her. "Ah sure do, ma'am," he said. "Ah think the act is ready to go on. The boys can play catch with Tom while I——"

"You are just wonderful," Keith's mother declared. "And that will give me a chance to get dinner ready."

"Please do," he said. "And remember, you promised pot roast and cornbread."

He followed Barbee out of the house and into the circle of admiring girls in her front yard.

"I'll get the mitts and ball," Keith said.

He could not wait to ask Tom why he had changed his attitude about their act. How come he was going to take part?

"Sonny wants it that way," the brother said. "He says everybody won't be so embarrassed if his own brother takes the lead in the pantomime."

Keith nodded. That made sense.

"That isn't all he said," Tom added, still rather tight-lipped. "He said the way to handle something like this is to walk right into it." He shook his head. He was upset still, that was evident. "Sonny said it's just like pitching a ball-game when the crowd is against you. You don't let them rattle you and you sure don't walk off the mound. You just rub resin on your fingers and throw that much harder." A sort of cold smile came to his face. "We'll make fun of Sonny Barton and I'll help you," he said slowly. "But remember he'll come back for an encore."

Keith frowned. He had not thought of that. "What'll he do then, make monkeys out of us?"

"No," Tom said firmly. "That's what I want him to do. But he'll do it his way. He always does."

"I sure hope he isn't mad," Keith sighed. "I wanted—well, gosh, I was hoping you could play in our league this year."

"You told me," grunted Tom. "About your manager having extra points, too. But Sonny doesn't see how that can be done. He is just booked here this week."

"But couldn't he get more jobs? Gosh, there are all sorts of supper clubs here. And your brother——"

"The fancy joints don't book him," Tom said tersely.

"They might," argued Keith. "Dick's dad owns the Villa Capri Motor Hotel and——"

Tom shook his dark head. "No chance." He could not keep the bitterness out of his voice. "The dinner crowd—Sonny is a honkey-tonk headliner."

Keith sighed. He saw that he might as well abandon that wild hope.

Exactly five hours later he turned and tossed on his bed, unable to sleep. What a night it had been! So many things to remember and to smile about. The first, the way Tom had thrown to Luke Doyle in their brief catch game. Luke had made the mistake of offering to catch their visitor. As a result, the freckle-faced boy had been forced to finger his guitar despite a blistered palm. Golly, how Tom had blazed that ball into Luke's mitt!

Then Mr. Gregg's first reaction to their dinner company. Have your lost your wits, he demanded of his wife? A honkey-tonk headliner eating at our table! She had quieted him with her explanation, but she had not appeased him. Well, he had finally grunted, he could understand her attitude. But the next time Mrs. Merrill had an idea——

Then the show. A packed house. Squealing girls filling the front rows. The terrible ordeal as Keith, Luke, and Dick took the first chorus alone, almost straight, only the lyrics revealing their intent. Then Sonny on the stage, his brother following as a sort of shadow, leading the *cavorting*, the grimaces, the exaggerated imitations.

Golly, gloated Keith, turning over in bed again, how the crowd had loved it——the grown-ups, that was. The feminine pack led by Barbee Brush had just sat there stunned and quiet. Some had broken into tears; Keith had heard their sobs above the singing.

Then Sonny alone after the round of hearty applause.

Sonny sitting on a stool waiting patiently for the noise to subside. Tom standing by Keith in the wing, features grim, eyes intent. Keith nervous, too, wondering what the singer would do now.

Quiet at last. Sonny's voice, calm and pleasant. "Ah'm glad you liked our act. The boys were quite good, weren't they?"

More applause, tempered with some protests from the front rows. Sonny's smile. "Ah would like to take them on tour with me. That was my little brother's first time on a stage. Ah had to make him go on. You can see that ah don't have all the ham in the family."

Keith was standing so close to Tom that he sensed the latter's tremble.

"Ah have had a good time myself. My brother, too. We were guests in a nice home and ah sure want to thank Mrs. Gregg for letting us join her family for an evening. That was a real treat for Tom and me. He is in the academy most of the year and ah don't have to tell you the life ah live. Tom got to play catch with some fine boys who played in your little league. He is growing up different from me—ah am seeing to that. He played little league last year and he made the all-star team as an eleven-year-old."

More applause. Keith looked at Tom. His lips were still tight and his eyes were a little moist.

Sonny took up his guitar. "Ah want to sing a song for Mrs. Gregg now," he said in that gentle tone. "My mother used to sing it to me. She started me singing, ah reckon; ah don't know who else did. It's a song ah haven't tried in a long time, but if you can put up with me—"

A long vamp. Keith had time to think about how Sonny

and Tom had feasted on his mother's cooking, how the former had praised it and Tom had nodded agreement.

The hall quieted as the swarthy entertainer showed a complete change of pace. This was a haunting song—a lullaby, guessed Keith.

"Turn around, turn around, and you are a wee child, a wee child asleep on my breast——"

Folk music, decided Keith. The rock-and-roll king singing a simple ballad. His voice as changed as his manner, too. Luke, who knew more about music than either of his two friends, said in an awed tone:

"Gosh, he can really sing!"

Keith shot a look at Tom. The younger Barton's features had relaxed slightly, even showed a small, set smile.

"Turn around, turn around, and you are a young man, a young man with a dream of your own."

So Sonny finished. A slight bow and a boyish grin, and loud, long applause, from the adults, the very people who had bought tickets only to indulge their children.

The singer sat still on his stool, waiting for the ovation to die down, that same smile on his face. Then, as quiet finally came, he said in the same calm way:

"But ah learned another thing from my mother. Many things, if even ah was just five when she died. My father never made much money, but he was never ashamed of what he did, nor my mother for him. And she taught me the same quality. Take what you are and do your best with it, and never be ashamed of it."

Then, without more warning, he was the regular Sonny Barton image, singing fiercely his rock-and-roll, cavorting with his own rhythm, eyes flashing. It sounded horrible to

Keith but he could not help listening. This, he was sure, was better than the usual Barton performance, too. And Tom stood watching, lips tight, eyes gleaming with pride.

The squealing from the teen-aged girls who had made this benefit show such a money-maker—Keith groaned as the chorus started and gained in volume. Then Sonny finished and he walked off the stage with a quick bow and for an instant he left a hushed audience behind him.

Keith re-smoothed his pillow and chuckled. He had felt just like his father. "I would say," Mr. Gregg had declared on the way home, "that our dinner guest crammed his rock-and-roll down our throats—and made us like it."

Keith's throat was suddenly parched. He slipped out of bed and down the stairway for a drink of water. He should be asleep, of course, but he could not quiet down.

For he had even more thrilling recollections of that busy evening.

The mob scene around Sonny, for instance, even by the adults. Richard Merrill had led the chorus of approval, Mr. Merrill who owned the Villa Capri and the Club Caravan which only booked the best perfomers.

"I had no idea you were so versatile, Sonny," he had said warmly. "I never heard that ballad before."

"Ah don't know that ah have ever heard anybody else sing it," the youth had said.

But most of his attention was claimed by the girls, of course. Hardly a one failed to offer an album for his autograph.

Mr. Gregg had wanted to leave but Keith's mother had refused. They must wait, she said, until she could invite

Sonny and Tom to dinner again. Keith caught his mother's elbow.

"Ask him about out little league."

"I will not," she whispered back. "I know better than to interfere with Mr. Tracy's team."

Keith sighed. Then he must do it himself.

The chance finally came. His mother thanked Sonny for dedicating the song to her.

"It was as sweet a ballad as I ever heard."

"I enjoyed it myself, very much," Mr. Gregg added. "The rock-and-roll, not much. But we are grateful to you, Sonny, very grateful."

"Ah enjoyed it. And ah know Tom did, too."

Tom was happy now, thought Keith. Tom stood proudly by his brother and matched Sonny's politeness.

Keith's opportunity at last.

"Sonny?"

"Yes, podner."

Keith licked his lips. "There's something I want to ask you."

"Shoot."

"About Tom?"

"What about him?"

"I sure wish he could play in our league this year. Couldn't you—you fixed it so he could play in Nashville last year?"

Tom was standing right there. "I told you how that was done," he said quickly. "Sonny had a contract with the Grand Old Opery and——"

"You ought to play somewhere," Sonny said slowly. "Ah

sure would hate for you to miss out on your twelfth year. You oughta really rise and shine this year."

"We have a good league," Keith said eagerly. "I hope Tom can get on my team. We have the smartest manager anywhere. But the other three coaches are good, too."

Sonny sighed. "Ah would have to fix up this residence business." He studied his brother. "How about it, Tom? Would you like to play in this league, if ah can arrange things?"

Tom said nothing for an instant, then took a deep breath. "I sure would," he said finally. "I would like to have these people eating out of my hand, just like you have."

Sonny's voice turned stern. "What did ah tell you about that?" he demanded.

Tom's eyes dropped. "Yes, Sonny," he said meekly.

"But you'd be happy playing here this summer?"

Tom nodded. "I sure would."

The singer nodded and turned to Keith's father. "You're a lawyer, aren't you, Mr. Gregg?"

"Of course, Sonny."

"Could ah talk to you tomorrow? Ah remember how much trouble it was last year—legal residence and all of that."

Mr. Gregg hesitated. "Yes, it is trouble, Sonny. I am also a director of the West Austin League and familiar with its regulations."

"Then you could be a real help to me. Could you come to my hotel in the morning?"

"Why not my office, Sonny?"

"If I came to your office, Mr. Gregg, I'd have girls and——"

"I know what you mean," Keith's father said with a smile. "And I don't want teen-agers swarming into our office. My partners would kill me. Is ten o'clock too early?"

"Just fine, sir." The singer smiled ruefully. "Ah don't usually get up that early. You just yank me out of bed."

"I'll help," Tom offered.

Keith slipped back up the stairs and to bed again. This time he fell asleep at once. Somehow he had a feeling that everything would work out, and that Tom Barton would solve the big pitching problem of the Atlas Giants.

CHAPTER 4

O

A Second Show-off

Dick said at first that he was tired of catch games. "Gosh, it's a whole week until practice starts. If we work out every day, we'll go stale."

"Nuts," scoffed Keith. "You ought to have been throwing all winter. You'll find how tough catching is. Wait until those Dodgers start running on you."

"You had better worry about yourself," Dick retorted. "I've seen you try to catch a fly ball. One of them is apt to hit you right on the head this year."

Keith did not deny that. He had never acquired the knack of judging a fly ball; he was sure himself that his only chance was at first base. And wearing the mitt loose on his hand, snatching the ball instead of taking it ker-plunk in a solid pocket—that was still unnatural.

"Sure," he admitted, "but I am willing to work. You'll never make a catcher until you get more desire."

He had learned to use the word "desire" from Darrell

Royal, head football coach of the University of Texas. The Longhorns had won the national championship the previous autumn and on his television shows Mr. Royal had said such stars as Duke Carlisle and Tommy Ford showed more desire than natural ability. Mr. Tracy usually said "hustle." We don't beat other teams, he repeated, we outhustle them.

"Oh, all right," Dick finally yielded. "We will throw a little while." A scowl came to his face. "But you got to quit acting like you're the coach of this team. Or even field captain. Mr. Tracy hasn't appointed you anything."

"I know that better than you do. The catcher ought to be the take-charge guy."

By then they had reached the intersection of Exposition Boulevard and Bonnie Road. Dick turned toward Keith's house. They were afoot; both lived so close to school that bicycles were more trouble than walking. A shout stopped them. Dave Parker and Joe Pettus came pedaling their bikes hard.

"A bunch is going to play work-up at West Enfield," Joe announced. "Get your gear and hustle down. Ruel is coming and Dave and maybe Doyle."

"We sure will," Keith said instantly. "Don't choose up 'til we get there."

"I don't have my bike," objected Dick.

"So you got to scoot home and get it," Keith snapped. "Make tracks. You need to run off some pounds anyhow."

"Nobody ever called you skinny."

But Dick started jogging at once. So did Keith, though he had less than a block to go.

Tom Barton sat waiting on the Gregg doorstep, pounding a new glove. Keith beamed.

"Hi," he said cordially.

"Hi."

"There's a work-up game at the playground. Want to play with us?"

"I guess so."

Keith hesitated. He had meant to ride his bike to the park and back; it was eight blocks with some uphill. But since Tom had no bicycle——

"Let me tell Mom and get my glove. Maybe she will drive us."

Mrs. Gregg agreed. "But don't let this get to be a habit," she warned. "I don't see the point of chauffeuring you somewhere and then you run yourself ragged. But I do want you to make our house your headquarters, Tom. My husband just called. He and your brother are still going over business."

"Yes, ma'am," nodded Tom. "Sonny was up early talking to his business manager in Nashville." He sighed. "That is Mr. Winthrop—most people call him 'Colonel.' He doesn't want Sonny to do this."

"But he will, won't he?" Keith asked anxiously.

"If he can manage it. Sonny doesn't always do what the Colonel wants." A smile danced across the swarthy features. "The Colonel calls Sonny a born lone wolf. That's some of the time. Other times he swells up like a toad and claims my brother is a spoiled brat."

"I would not say that," Mrs. Gregg said quickly.

"If he wants to live here—this Colonel can't stop him?"

"It's a matter of bookings," said Tom with a shrug.

"Sonny can cut his records here, though the Colonel doesn't like that either."

"Why not?"

"Accompaniment and arrangement. Sonny always uses a full background."

"It is complicated," Mrs. Gregg nodded. "My husband said that as fast as they settled one problem, two others showed up."

"We ought not to try it," Tom muttered. Then his eyes glinted. "But I sure hope we can. I want to have a real good season. Then next year I can play on the academy. You have to be in the ninth grade before——"

"You will be in the ninth grade?" marveled Keith.

"Starting in August," Tom said lightly. "I'm a year ahead."

Now they had reached the playground. A dozen or so boys were flipping balls back and forth and Keith saw two others approaching afoot.

"Golly, we can have a real game," he gloated.

The waiting group included most of the league's better players—Ruel Snead and Mike Levy of Calumet, Doyle Chandler and Tobin Wingo of the Reds, Marty Kuhlman and Rene Ramirez of the Dodgers. Dick and Luke came riding up on their bicycles almost immediately.

Keith was awkward about introducing Tom; he had no experience in such formalities. He was prepared for some wisecracks about Tom's brother, but none came, not in actual words. The feeling was there, though; Tom Barton was not too welcome. He sensed it, too, or perhaps he even started it by his own attitude. He kept away from the argument about organizing their game. Ruel insisted that

they swap defensive positions at will instead of following
the usual pattern of moving from outfield to third base and
on around. Let each pitcher throw a full inning, he said,
and the catchers take turns behind the plate.

"None of us will get any real practice if we don't,"
argued the Calumet pitcher.

That suited Keith; he wanted to play first base. Rene
disagreed. The pitchers would throw too hard, he claimed,
and the hitters would get little or no practice. Nobody's
batting eye was sharp. Mr. Collins usually had them swinging against the machine until they had grooved their
swings. He believed the pitchers were ahead of the hitters
in development instead of lagging behind, as in professional baseball. Sneaker Kane of Calumet believed exactly
the opposite. The Cats did not face the mechanical throwing arm at any time.

"We could argue 'til dark and get nowhere," Dan Poggin
pointed out. "Let's swap around on defense and the pitchers throw two-thirds speed, like in regular batting practice."

That suited most of the boys; the minority yielded gracefully. The important thing was to get playing.

Their number had swelled to fourteen when they drew
for batting turns. Five hitters in bat at a time—that was
easy to settle. A batter stayed in until put out, then went to
the bottom of the hitting list. A caught fly would be just
another out, not an automatic change between batter and
fielder.

Tom Barton had not said anything during all of this,
acting as if these details were unimportant.

Ruel took the first mound turn with Dick behind the
plate, using Tobin's mask, mitt, and protectors. Ruel assigned his defense.

"What do you play?" he asked Tom.

"Pitch and short usually."

Ruel hesitated. He had already assigned both positions. "How about outfield?"

"Anywhere," Tom said carelessly.

"Then take center."

Tom ran to the post without comment. Keith looked after him a bit anxiously. He sure had none of his brother's stage personality. Sonny, in a crowd, was all smiles and polite talk; Tom showed no friendliness at all. Was it shyness, Keith wondered, or some other sort of feeling? Could Tom Barton be thinking that because of his experience with a successful tournament team that he was better than his new associates? If so, then he might have a lesson in store for him. The West Austin Little League produced strong teams year after year. One of their all-star units had actually made it to Williamsport, and all the way to the final round. Mr. Tracy had coached that team, too.

Keith was the second batter. He chose the lightest of the four used bats and took practice swings while Ruel pitched to Tobin Wingo. The Winston catcher hit a sharp grounder which the shortstop bobbled. This infield was rough; more ground balls would be missed than fielded.

Tobe was safe at first and Keith stepped in. He was a good hitter and his father had taken him to public cages throughout the winter. Both of his parents shared his concern about this final little league season. It would not be easy for him to learn another position; he had caught since his ninth year, through the Pee-wee and minor league and right up to regular receiver for the Giants at eleven. His improvement at the plate, agreed Mr. Gregg, could settle any doubt as to his winning another starting assignment. Just hit five hundred, said his father, and Jim Tracy will play you somewhere. A good hitter has never been kept on the bench in this league.

Keith squarely met the second offering. He was not a power swing but a line drive hitter. He had learned to hit to the opposite field last year, too; the opposition usually played him straight away.

His drive went to right center. Wingo ran with the bat's crack. Tobe rounded second at full speed. A runner should be able to take third on such a long single.

But the slim swarthy boy in center field moved with catlike quickness. He fielded the drive on the bounce and threw to third without a second's hesitation. Keith headed for second without stopping, sure of being safe.

But Tom's peg was right into Luke's glove. Tobin was so surprised that he did not think to slide. He was tagged out two steps from the base and Luke fired to Steve Kalumas at second. Keith hit the dirt but it was no use. The ball was slapped against his thigh and the improvised infield yelped with glee as it went around the horn.

"Gosh," gloated Steve, "we are looking like an all-star team."

Keith shook his head ruefully and swapped positions with Doyle Chandler.

"Tough luck," said the Winston star. He hesitated. "That Barton kid—he ate that up. He can play center field for me. Somebody has worked with him as an outfielder."

"He claims to be a pitcher," Keith muttered, disgusted at losing his batting turn so quickly. A clean hit if he had just held up at first! But who wouldn't have tried for second? He looked out toward center field. Tom still showed that same lack of facial expression. He acted as if he did not even hear the compliments of his fellow fielders, as if such plays were usual with him. Keith grunted and remembered Tom's explanation. He meant to develop into an all-around player and let his college coach decide whether he should pitch or fill another position. Well, Tom Barton could pitch and play center field. How was he at the plate? If he could hit as well as he threw and fielded, then he was almost a ball club himself.

But he couldn't. His turn with the bat came shortly and he struck out. Dan Poggin was pitching by then and, while Dan was a stout pitcher, the Winston ace did not bear down. Keith kicked up dust at first base as Tom picked up his glove and ran back to center field. Anybody was apt to fan, of course, even against this sort of pitching, especially if this was his first time to swing this season. Keith's own batting eye, he must remember, had been kept sharp by those batting cage sessions.

But several things warned him that Tom Barton was not so good with the stick. His batting stance, for one thing— foot in the bucket. Mr. Tracy insisted no boy could hit until he learned to anchor his back foot. Tom jerked his head, too; it had seemed so to Keith anyhow. And batters with that fault were suckers for low pitches, either close or on the outside corner. But Tom's own attitude had been more revealing. He did not act surprised or appear disgruntled in the least.

But field, golly—Rene took the mound and Tom moved to shortstop in the general shift of defensive positions. A grounder was hit sharply to him by Mart Kuhlman. The ball took a bad hop as could be expected on this field. The best Tom could do was knock it down. He snatched it quickly and his peg burned Keith's palm—he had forgotten and let the mitt slip down over his hand. Mart was out by a full step.

Then, after several more outs, Tom requested his chance to pitch, the first words he had spoken. Louis Chastain of the Cats yielded the mound; Tom took five quick warm-up throws and nodded that he was ready.

Keith sighed. He had hoped to keep Tom's hurling ability as much of a secret as possible just in case Sonny Barton could settle this legal residence business. But there was no doubting that this particular cat could not be kept in a bag.

Tom's first pitch proved that. Joe Pettus swung late and Joe was a fairly good hitter. He struck out on four pitches and grumbled to himself as he went to second base.

Keith knew what his Giant teammate was thinking— Tom Barton was bearing down harder than the other hitters. Not throwing with all he had, perhaps, but certainly not holding to any two-thirds speed.

Rene and Ruel fared no better. The latter managed a weak rolling foul; otherwise none of Tom's offerings were touched by the bat.

Twilight was closing in; nobody objected when Ruel proposed they quit.

"I'll walk home with you and call a taxi," Tom said to Keith. "If that's all right, of course."

Keith nodded. "Sure. Maybe my mother or my dad will drive you where——"

"No," was the firm answer. "Sonny said to call a taxi."

"Let me get a drink first," Keith said, joining the group at the concrete fountain.

Ruel, Louis, and Rene were talking about Tom as they waited their turns.

"Is he living here now?" demanded Ruel, nodding toward Tom, who was standing off alone.

"He may be," Keith admitted. "His brother is trying to fix that up."

"Then he will eligible for the league?"

"Sure," spoke up Luke Doyle. "Keith and Dick—they wanted to keep it quiet. They hoped to slip him in as a ringer."

"Well, they won't," Rene declared. "If Mr. Tracy gets him, he will have to pay for him. This kid can play ball, even if he is as big a show-off as his brother."

Keith did not dispute that. He could not deny that his new friend had made a point of his pitching prowess—too much so considering that Ruel, Rene, and the other pitchers had not tried for strikeouts. Keith was disappointed with Tom's attitude, too. He sure hadn't tried to be friendly; he did not seem to care whether the other boys liked him or not. And that was not the way in the West Austin League. They played to beat each other and many of them cried when they lost ballgames, especially if the championship was at stake. But that rivalry was left on the diamond. It sure never interfered with their association off the field. Take him and Luke, for instance—they had played on different teams since their eighth year. And last season the playoff between Atlas and Calumet had been decided by a close play at the plate. Most of the Cats still claimed they had suffered from a hasty decision.

There was little talk as he and Tom trudged home. Mrs. Gregg telephoned for a taxi after firm refusal of her offer to drive Tom to the downtown hotel. The cab came and left before Mr. Gregg returned home. He had had a hard day, he sighed, sinking into his favorite chair.

"I am happy to have a new client, of course," he sighed, "but I had no idea what I was in for. I am not dealing with just one seventeen-year-old boy, but a corporation. A rock-and-roll king is big business. We are having to incorporate under Texas laws as a subsidiary of the Nashville office."

"Can it be arranged?" Mrs. Gregg put the question; Keith waited anxiously for his father's verdict.

"It *will* be done," said Mr. Gregg. His eyes twinkled at his wife. "You favorite singer is also a sharp and strong-willed businessman. I have no intention of ever managing any artist, but if it should come to that, I will draw the line against Sonny Barton."

"Tom can play in our league then?" asked Keith. He was not sure he understood what his father was talking about.

"I am willing to predict that," nodded the lawyer. He shifted his weight. "After a hundred or so more long distance calls, procurement of a charter from the Secretary of State, and a few more details—I would say Tom can play through the first half anyhow."

"Just the first half!" Keith's face fell. Who wanted a star pitcher for just half the season? What good would it do to earn a place in the playoff and then be without your mound ace for the showdown game?

"Perhaps all season," said Mr. Gregg. "This seventeen-year-old dynamo is already booked in this area for the next eight weeks. If there were more honkey-tonks or teen-age dance spots, he could work here and in nearby cities the rest of his life. He doesn't *ask* for engagements, nor trust his manager to do it. He just calls up the manager that week and says he's available. If the manager has another booking for those nights—well, just cancel them." He smiled faintly. "And I am to lease him an apartment within the league's area tomorrow. With a swimming pool, of course, nothing but the best." He hesitated, then studied his son. "Is he worth all this trouble, Keith—as a ball player, I mean?"

"Tom?"

"Yes."

Keith licked his lips. "He can pitch," he said slowly. "Maybe he can outpitch anybody this league ever had. Field, too—outfield, shortstop—anywhere, I guess. But I don't look for him to hit much and—"

"And what?" asked Mrs. Gregg.

Keith lowered his head. "Well, he is sort of—I don't know how to say it."

"I think I do," stated the lawyer. "I observed him some this morning. That boy has a chip on his shoulder. He won't prove an easy boy to handle."

"Jim Tracy can handle any boy," Mrs. Gregg declared.

"Maybe," said Keith's father. "But I am sure even Jim Tracy has his limitations."

CHAPTER 5

O

Is He a Prize Package?

It was done. Mr. Gregg announced that at lunch, adding that he meant to rest that afternoon. He was tired of paper work, he said, and needed a relaxing round of golf.

Keith could not help chortling. Tom Barton could play!

"That has been confirmed by the league president," said his father. "All conditions have been met. Sonny would not let me rest until everything was fully settled."

"But can he play all season?" asked Mrs. Gregg.

"I don't see how he can. Sonny has a big overhead expense and, of course, most of his earnings go for income tax. His manager does not believe the summer business in Texas is big enough for such fees, and I agree—though certainly I am no authority on night spots and supper clubs."

"What is wrong with summer?" asked Keith.

"College enrollments drop off, familes take vacations, many people prefer the outdoors." The lawyer smiled ruefully. "Unless their sons are playing little league baseball, of course. Then they devote May, June, and July to that."

"He will play all year," predicted Keith. "And if Dick can just learn to catch him——"

"I would not count too strongly on Mr. Tracy picking him," Mrs. Gregg cautioned her son. "I talked with him at the community center this morning. He has heard of this new prospect, but he seems skeptical. He said he might emphasize younger boys and build a team for next year or the season after that."

"That is his usual strategy," nodded Mr. Gregg. He was speaking from his experience as players' agent, a post to which he had been re-elected. "Jim Tracy and Chase Alloway believe in taking boys young and training them from scratch. According to league talk, Mac Collins usually outbids his rivals for the twelve-year-old prizes."

"Gosh, he has Rene Ramirez and Billy Harper," Keith protested. "The Dodgers don't need a twelve-year-old pitcher. A shortstop neither. Tom McMillan is plenty good."

"That's in his favor as far as young Barton is concerned."

"Why?"

"Say Tom can play only the first half. Mac's team would not be wrecked by such a sudden loss. Whereas your Giants——"

"And Mr. Tracy is doubtful about Dick Merrill," broke in Mrs. Gregg. "If it's any consolation to you, son, your manager considers that your accident just about ruined his pennant chances."

"Dick will come through," Keith said. "I'll see to that."

He sighed. "But even with Tom," he reflected, "we will need another pitcher. Maybe I can make it as a sidearmer."

"If you could develop control——"

"That's the trouble. I throw hard enough, but—gosh, I don't know where the ball is going." His lips tightened. "But I will be throwing all right by the first game. So will Dick."

The telephone interrupted their meal. "For you, son," announced Mrs. Gregg. "Tom, I think."

So it was. "Grab your bathing trunks and hustle over," he said excitedly. "We have the fanciest swimming pool you ever saw."

"I can't do that. My mother would——"

"Ask her," urged the singer's brother. "Ask her right now."

Keith did, though he was sure what she would say. "In early April! I should say not."

"The calendar has nothing to do with it," explained Mr. Gregg. "I have leased the Barton brothers an apartment at the Regal Arms. It has an indoor pool, heated. Your favorite singer goes first class, my dear."

"I never thought of that," said Keith's mother.

"Then I can go?"

"An hour after your lunch," she relented. "And it isn't far; you can go on your bicycle."

"Or walk," Keith said, hurrying back to the telephone. The Regal Arms was less than four blocks away, set back among stately oaks. Keith had heard it described as the most expensive apartment unit in Austin. He promised to be there in an hour.

"But if he earns so much, why doesn't he cut expenses and save——"

His mother was saying that when Keith returned to the table.

"He is saving," Mr. Gregg said. "He has two trust funds, one for Tom and another for himself. I suppose your protégé could live comfortably if he never cut another record."

"Then why does he drive himself so hard? The poor boy must——"

"He is anything but poor. He was born that way but rock-and-roll swept him right to the top."

"He has a nice voice," she mused. "When he sang that lullaby—I had goose bumps all over."

"He was pleased with the response, if that makes you feel any better. He intends to include a folk song in his repertory from now on." Mr. Gregg pushed back his chair and his eyes twinkled at his wife and son. "I have made both of you happy," he said, "and I humbly ask permission to indulge myself this afternoon. Have a good time in the heated pool, son. But don't let such luxury go to your head."

Keith grinned. He wouldn't.

He and Tom were splashing in the heated water by two o'clock. Keith suggested that Tom invite Dick to share in the fun but Tom shook his head.

"Later maybe," he said. "Sonny said never to ask too many." His eyes clouded. "The manager didn't want to take us in. He said he leased to your dad without knowing who would live in the place. Sonny had to promise never to rehearse here." He sighed. "This is sure the snooty part of town, isn't it?"

Keith supposed that was true; he had heard the same charge many times. His own mother had admitted it more than once. But she called it an "exclusive" neighborhood rather than snobby. And Mr. Gregg had said once, trying to explain the feeling about newcomers, that it was a question of protecting property values. So social "standards" kept prices higher. No vacant lot was ever sold without restrictions as to type of house and minimum cost. And each residence had to be set back at least seventy-five feet from the street.

"You and your brother don't have to worry," Keith said. "He makes more money maybe than anybody who lives out here."

"He does," Tom said proudly, "and we are just as good as anybody, too—Sonny at singing and me at baseball. I guess I proved that yesterday."

Keith scowled. Tom had flouted the usual spirit of such work-up games. "You bore down harder than Ruel or Rene," he said. "You will face batters in this league who can hit you. My dad has been taking me to batting cages all winter and I am ready for fast pitching right now. Try striking me out if you think you can just throw the ball by anybody in this league."

"I think I could," said Tom with a smile, "but I won't try it. I wouldn't throw as hard to you as the other hitters."

"Why not? What if you end up on another team? Mac Collins, for instance."

Tom shook his head. "I wouldn't want that. I want to be on your team."

"You know how tryouts go—and player auctions."

"But you said your coach has points from last year—he can outbid the others."

"He could," Keith admitted. "But will he?" Keith's lips tightened. "You had better change your tune, I'll tell you that. Mr. Tracy doesn't like cocky boys."

Tom smiled. "But he likes to win championships. Your Jim Tracy has won more times than the other managers put together."

"Who told you that? My dad?"

"No. Sonny wanted to be sure I played for a competent manager this season. He doesn't trust the average little league coach. He wanted to be sure I would get something out of playing this year."

Keith grunted. "You and he talk like you're a big league prospect already."

"I am," Tom said calmly. "Or close to it."

"You can talk yourself right off Mr. Tracy's team if you aren't careful. With you leaving at the half, and—well, he may not even bid on you."

A scowl covered the swarthy features. "You haven't told him that, have you?"

"He knows it already," Keith's lips tightened. "But I would have told him. I think he should know before the auction. The other managers, too."

"Sonny has cancelled all bookings except close to Austin," Tom said coldly. "He will sing out of here as long as he can get engagements. And that might last a whole year—if he wants it. He doesn't ask for jobs; he tells managers when he is available to them."

Keith sighed. So his father had said.

"But what about the summer slump? My dad said——"

"It won't happen, with Sonny performing."

"You got it all figured out," Keith said disgustedly. "But it might not go that way. You're not that good a ball player in the first place."

"You'll see," Tom said with his quick, flashing smile. "Your Mr. Tracy will be convinced in tryouts. He will go to that auction with his mind made up to outbid anybody and everybody."

"Then you'd better come over to my house and throw every day."

"To you?"

"No, to Dick. If you pitch for us, you'll have him as a receiver."

Tom Barton scowled. "He can't hold me. I saw that the other day. He can't move fast enough to take a curve."

"If he can't learn," shrugged Keith, "then it will just be too bad. Because Dick is our only catching hope, especially if Mr. Tracy *does* get you. He won't have the points left to pick up a catcher, too, even if there is a good one coming up from the minors. And there usually isn't." He started to add that he had been one of the few West Austin boys to step right out of the minor league and into a starting position in the major circuit. And that had been mainly because of his strong peg, which he no longer boasted.

"Will Dick let me coach him?" demanded Tom. "I can catch. My manager would have used me behind the plate last year if he had not wanted me at shortstop when I wasn't pitching."

Keith sighed. He could not be sure how Dick would react to Tom's directions. The blond-headed boy lacked the driving desire of Keith, or of Ruel Snead, and apparently of Tom Barton.

"Maybe he will listen," he mused. "But you need to work on something yourself. I can show you things about batting."

Tom admitted that. "I don't hit my weight," he sighed. He shook his dark head. "I guess that will make me a pitcher and nothing else. Pitchers don't have to hit."

"They do in this league. Ruel and Rene bat third or fourth all of the time."

"I am willing to try," Tom said in a different tone. "I *want* to hit, believe me."

"You can do anything you want to," Keith said firmly. "Look at me—having to learn to throw all over again. But I'll do it. I'll play first base or somewhere this year, but I'll be back catching in a year or two."

"Sure you will." Tom nodded and his lips twitched. "I never had a friend like you, Keith," he added slowly, each word seeming to come as an effort. "I guess, to tell the truth, you are the first real friend I ever had."

Keith ducked his head. What could he say to that? He took a deep breath. "Let's dress and find Dick," he said a bit gruffly. "You got to really go some to get Mr. Tracy excited about you. And Dick—well, I just don't know. Mr. Tracy isn't sure of him at all."

"He handles the mitt, all right. He just doesn't shift his weight——"

"Don't tell me," said Keith. "I've been after him about that all winter. Let's find him—then can he come back here for a swim? He'd get as much kick out of this heated pool——"

"Of course," Tom agreed. "I will ask him myself—every day until the season starts. Then we quit, of course. I am sure Mr. Tracy won't let us mix swimming and baseball."

"You're counting your chickens before they hatch," Keith warned again.

"No," denied Tom. "I learned that from my brother. You don't just wait for eggs to hatch anymore. You put them into an incubator and set the temperature and the chicks are born the day you want them."

Keith sighed. There was no point of arguing with this swarthy boy. He had learned all the answers from his brother.

Keith had been through two West Austin tryouts, so was surprised by neither the swarm of candidates nor the well organized procedure. The league president, Mr. Don Thomas, gave out instructions over the public address system. Keith's father sat at a table checking applications and issuing numbers. A dozen adults stood waiting to put the several groups through tests of hitting, fielding, and running.

Keith smiled as he recalled his feelings of last year—that the managers themselves seemed to keep out of the tryout picture. He knew better now, of course. He was one of seven boys picked by Mr. Tracy to help judge the new hopefuls and to contact those who showed promise. Mr. Tracy himself knelt in left field with Mr. Dudley, his assistant manager. Each had a clipboard and a full listing of all candidates, including their assigned numbers.

Joe, Dave Parker, Roy Murray, Davis Gordon, Jackie LeClerc, and Dick—they waited as eagerly as Keith, and as proud of their new responsibility. They would help pick the seven new players to wear the Atlas blue. The Cats, Reds, and Dodgers—their groups were as ready, too. And Keith could be sure that the other managers had collected as much advance information as Mr. Tracy. Most of these hundred and seventy candidates had played in the minor league last year; their batting and fielding records were there for quick reference. And the Giants' returning veterans had given Mr. Tracy their written opinions as to the abilities, personalities, and even personal ideas about the better prospects.

For this human mill was no disorganized business, no matter how it looked to the anxious parents watching from stands and behind the fences.

A dozen or so more boys were already spotted, probably on every manager's list. Dave Baker, Frank Holmes, Bart French, Joe Weiman, Duke Canfield—these were ready to "move up." Keith had said so; his teammates had agreed.

"You have to be on the inside to realize how fair and efficient these tryouts are," Mr. Gregg had told his wife that morning. "I would never have known it if I hadn't become players' agent. This league will take in twenty-eight new boys. Each manager makes his nomination without any sort of check with the others before the auction. But probably no more than forty names will even come up. There is little or no guesswork to it."

"That should be explained to the worrying parents," Mrs. Gregg had answered. "I know how they feel—that the managers pay little attention to their sons. I sat through two of those tryouts, you know, and I was sick after both. And I was very unhappy when Keith did not get a uniform the second time. I was sure he hadn't been given a fair trial and I said so."

"You sure did," Mr. Gregg had smiled. "You complained last year, too—to anybody who would listen. And, all the time, down on the field in the middle of it, I realized that all four managers were interested in Keith."

"I will never forgive you for not telling me so."

"Watch the boys back from last year, the ones in their team camps," Mr. Gregg had explained. "They streak after any boy who has caught their manager's eye. And when two or more dart for the same boy, you can count him in."

Keith remembered well what had happened after his turn at bat the previous spring. He had "run out" his second bunt according to instructions and had found four boys waiting for him when he passed first base, including Merle Conroy of the Giants. Merle had put in first claim for Keith's attention. "Mr. Tracy wants me to throw to you," the pitcher had said gruffly. "Here's a mitt; come on."

Keith had followed obediently. Then others had claimed their turns. He had crouched in the right field corner, catching a hundred throws, but never—as far as he could tell—receiving any manager's personal attention.

Mr. Tracy gave last instructions to his "scouts."

"We want speed and throwing," he said, "and especially ten-year-olds. Jacques, you grab this Abe Duran. I hear he can hit and use a glove."

"Yes, sir," Jacques LaClerc said.

"Can I wait for Tom Barton so we can have him first?" Keith asked eagerly. It was first come first served after a candidate finished his batting turn.

"No point in it," the tall manager said lightly. "Let the other managers stew over Barton. We have a full report on him already." His gray eyes twinkled. "You wrote almost a book yourself," he reminded Keith.

So Keith had. He had been fair, too, to the best of his ability. Tom could be the league's outstanding pitcher, he had declared, its best fielding shortstop and probably its standout catcher. But, putting team loyalty ahead of personal feeling, he had also listed possible weaknesses—weak hitting and uncertainty as to how long his brother could live in West Austin.

Keith wondered again what Dick had reported about Tom. Joe Pettus, too. Both had refused to say. Joe's opinion, brooded Keith, would have more influence than Dick's. Mr. Tracy thought highly of his second baseman; Joe might even be appointed field captain.

Mr. Dudley made most of the additional notations. First in the speed tests—Tom Barton. Abe Duran a poor seventh.

"I thought he was faster than that," said Mr. Tracy.

"He is," claimed Joe. "He got off to a poor start."

Keith ducked his head to hide his expression. Joe lived across the street from Abe Duran; the two were close friends. According to Keith's findings, Abe had proven only an average shortstop in minor league play.

The fielding—both of fly balls and in improvised infield combinations.

Barton again. Keith was not sure whether to be pleased or not. The better Tom's showing, the higher the price tag in spite of the doubt that he could play a full season. Still, he mused, such a pitcher might mean the difference in first half competition.

That was all that could be crowded into the first day's schedule. Hitting the second day, two bunts after five cuts, then individual tests as the managers wished.

Keith knew what to expect of Tom at the plate—nothing. He missed three slings from the machine and dribbled off two others. His bunts—one was wide of the baseline, the other a good effort. He did not square around in the usual little league manner, instead poked at the ball with small change in his stance.

"Used to dragging," Keith heard Mr. Dudley mutter. "We don't see much of that."

Tom ran out the second bunt and was immediately collared by runners from Winston, Bedford, and Calumet. Keith looked anxiously to Mr. Tracy. Had he decided against even bidding for the singer's brother? Wasn't the Giant manager even interested in seeing how Tom pitched? Mac Collins of the Dodgers sure was. Marty Kuhlman was leading Tom into deep center field. Marty had his mitt, of course. And now Mr. Collins was walking over from the Bedford huddle for closer appraisal. Louis Chastain of the Cats and Tobe Wingo of the Reds were standing right behind the crouching Marty.

Keith studied Mr. Tracy's lean features again, then heaved a sigh which set his full frame to trembling. He had done all he could, he thought unhappily. And he could not deny that his parents had tried to brace him for this blow. Mr. Tracy had said he would probably pick the best of the younger candidates and build for the future.

"Put Duran first on our list," Mr. Tracy told his assistant

manager. "I am guessing he can play third for us this year and back up Dick behind the plate. Maybe even beat Merrill out."

Keith bit his lips. He believed the tall manager was overestimating Abe as a prospect. Probably, he thought unhappily, and with some bitterness, Joe Pettus had built up his friend.

CHAPTER 6

O

Mr. Tracy Accepts a Challenge

The auction was that night. Mr. Gregg did not even come home for dinner. He would grab a sandwich, he said, then re-check all applications to league age and eligibility.

"And don't expect me home early," he warned his wife. "This bidding goes slowly. The first offer has to be for two hundred and fifty points, but fifty-point bids can be made after that. And sometimes the most interested manager does not speak up until the bidding gets high."

Keith better understood the auction process than most boys because of such comments by his father. Each manager was allowed ten thousand points a season to "buy" new players. Any unused points carried over into the next year, as did any deficits. Thus Mr. Tracy's point surplus this season—he had not used his full allotments in the last two auctions. And, Keith had learned, Mac Collins had only nine thousand points to "invest" this year. He had an "option player" on his squad—a boy he had taken last year who would be charged against his next "balance."

So Mr. Tracy could easily outbid Mac for Tom Barton. But the Giants would put up Abe Duran first—didn't that mean Mr. Tracy meant to "pay" whatever it took to acquire the stocky infielder?

"You cannot do a thing about it," Mrs. Gregg advised her son as Keith voiced his unhappiness. She hesitated, then added: "I can tell you this. Tom made a bad impression on the onlookers, at least. I heard several comments about his sullen expression and his cocksureness. He acted as if the tryouts were just foolishness."

"He wasn't nervous like the other kids," Keith said in quick defense of his friend. "He was an all-star player last year—pitched in the state finals. Why should he pretend to be scared or excited, or to doubt that he would make a team?"

"I understand that. But he has a chip on his shoulder and you could see that from the stands. And he doesn't get along well with the other boys—that is general knowledge."

Keith sighed. He could not deny that. Dick Merrill had come right out and said that he hoped Tom would be picked on another team. But Dick had some things to learn himself. It might shake the towhead up some to learn that Mr. Tracy wanted Abe Duran as a possible starting catcher rather than a third baseman. Dick was a doubtful starter and had nobody but himself to blame. He complained that Keith and Tom were "riding him" where all they wanted was to help him.

But it was out of Keith's hands, that was for sure. He finished his homework, watched a television show indifferently, then went to bed. He tossed and turned awhile, then fell sound asleep.

His mother awoke him next morning instead of his father. The auction had lasted until past two, she explained; Mr. Gregg intended to sleep late.

"Did he say anything about the bidding?"

"I didn't see him. He just left a note. Now eat your breakfast and hustle off to school. We are running late as it is."

They were indeed. The bell rang as Keith reached the school building.

Nobody knew anything of the player selections—he asked a dozen boys and was asked by as many in turn. The complete list would be published in the Sunday newspaper but official practice started that very afternoon. The new players would be out, of course, informed of their teams and practice sites by telephone. But such messages would not reach them until after school. Until then——

Keith learned about one new teammate, Abe. His family had an unlisted telephone. Mr. Tracy had left a note in the Pettus mailbox for Joe to get Abe out for practice that afternoon.

"He won't help us much," Dick said when told of this by Keith. "He played short and first mostly and—shucks, he can't field like Jacques or hit like you."

"He can catch, too," Keith said coldly, "and he has a good arm. I heard Mr. Tracy say he might start Abe in your place."

Dick studied his friend. "You're kidding."

"I am not. I've tried to tell you and so has Tom. You can't just slap at the ball. And you can't take two steps before you peg."

"You and Barton," grunted Dick. "I'll do the catching for Atlas this year. You worry about who will play first base."

Keith managed to slip into the attendance office during physical training and use the telephone, but got only the busy signal from the Barton apartment. Sonny and his bookings, he grumbled to himself, remembering his father's description of how the singer made long distance calls.

Three o'clock finally came. Keith hurried out of the school building, but still Dick overtook him within a block.

"Mrs. Baker brought David his cap and glove," said the towhead. "He went to Winston."

"We could have used him," Keith regretted.

"She said the Reds got Duke Canfield."

Another choice to rue, according to Keith's evaluations. He had recommended Duke to Mr. Tracy.

The Giants would practice at Knebel Field. Both Keith and Dick had worn their caps to school and had brought their gloves. They cut through the municipal golf course, the shortest route to the park.

They were the first there but others came shortly—all of the veterans, happy, talking loudly and excitedly. And the new players, quieter and less sure of themselves, but plainly thrilled with their lot. It would have been wonderful to have been picked by any manager, but by Jim Tracy— super, super! They acted still a little dazed by their good fortune.

Keith counted them off—Abe, Joe Weiman, Miles

Carowe, José Aguirre, Pat Maguire, Tim Haley—only six so far—eleven-year-old Abe and five youngsters aged ten. Mr. Tracy had sure meant his words about concentrating on young players. But who was the seventh addition? Keith pointed this out to Joe; the second baseman shook his head. He had no idea.

Then Keith saw his mother's car pulling to a stop outside the locked gate. Why? She had known he would go straight from school to practice. And he had remembered everything, even to thick cotton socks.

She was letting a boy out, that was why she had come. And that boy——

Keith whooped in delight. He had never seen the crimson cap before, but he recognized its wearer at once.

Tom Barton! He vaulted the low chain link fence and came to the dugout at a trot. Keith ran to meet him.

"You're on our team!"

A grin flitted across Tom's olive features. "Didn't I tell you I would be?"

"Sure, but Mr. Tracy—he didn't seem the least bit——"

"He called Sonny about ten o'clock. They talked quite a while—I don't know what all they had to say. I caught a taxi to your house, thinking you would go home first. Besides I didn't know how to find this field. Your mother was sweet enough to bring me and——"

The arrival of Mr. Dudley stopped further talk. A quick lap, ordered the assistant manager. He was a strapping young man who had caught in college baseball. He helped Mr. Tracy with every phase of practice but took almost complete charge of the receivers. He was a hard taskmaster, too; Keith grinned as he thought of the trying summer in store for Dick Merrill, especially with Abe Duran as a challenger.

They had started out almost even the year before, Keith and Dick. But Keith had won Mr. Dudley's early approval with his hustle and had improved steadily all season.

It might be the same way this year, brooded Keith. Mr. Dudley was less patient than Mr. Tracy. If Dick didn't change his attitude——

"Around the field again," ordered Mr. Dudley, "and this time on the double. Sweat the candy and soda pop out of your carcasses."

Keith knew enough to run this time, not trot. So did most of the others and only one newcomer failed to follow suit. Mr. Dudley stood waiting for Tom Barton as the swarthy boy jogged up to the dugout.

"Another one, Barton," the assistant manager said curtly. "Maybe ten more, unless you run. We don't trot or walk anywhere on this team."

Tom scowled but obeyed. Mr. Tracy, now coming through the gate, asked no questions about the lone boy circling the field. Instead he had Joe and Dave roll out the pitching machine and Abe don the catching equipment.

"All new boys in to bat," he ordered. "You old heads, take your regular position. At first, Gregg."

"Yes, sir," Keith said quickly. Mr. Tracy followed him with a fungo. The infield was complete except for a third baseman. Tom was sent there, to Keith's surprise. Shouldn't Tom be at shortstop?

But he had better worry about first base, he decided. The ball was coming around the horn; Keith took a peg from

Jac and threw home. Toward home, rather; his sidearmed effort was high and wide.

He looked ruefully to Mr. Tracy. "You will throw many a wild one to start with," the manager said lightly. "Take a little more time."

Keith nodded.

Infield, outfield, and hitting at the same time—Mr. Tracy did not believe in wasting a minute of practice. Not regular infield, of course; he hit balls and the fielders threw to first only. The manager stopped twice to show Keith how to reach for the ball, how to shift his feet according to each throw. He wanted the ball caught in front of the base.

"The umpire is usually watching the runner's foot," he explained, "and listening for the ball to hit the mitt. Taking the throw out an arm's reach—that way you cost the runner a half step. And a lot of plays are that close at first."

"Yes, sir," Keith said, grateful for this close, patient attention. He remembered what Mr. Tracy had said of Bob Lockett the year before—a first baseman could be developed in one season. All it took was size and effort.

A peg from Jacques sailed wide; Mr. Tracy scolded Keith for not leaving the bag.

"Never give them an extra base," he said. "Hold the bag if you can, but don't mind leaving it. It isn't your error if the runner gets first on a poor throw. But if he goes on to second—then you're to blame. You've let him get into scoring position."

"Yes, sir," Keith said again.

On and on went the calm reprimands. You could have stretched for that one, Gregg. And you have to play those in the dirt, too. Go down for them. Let the ball hit you in the chest or even your face. First basemen aren't supposed to look pretty. Nothing gets through you or by you, just like catching.

Catching—Abe Duran was getting the same type of coaching from Jack Dudley. Keith heard snatches of the assistant manager's talk. Move your feet, Duran. Don't stand there rooted like a tree. And dive into the low ones. Block everything. That is why you have shin guards, chest protector, and a mask.

Dick was in the outfield and occasionally Mr. Tracy lifted a fly without warning. He followed no routine with his fungo; in fact, he tried to catch boys not watching. And any offender went around the field. Dave Parker first, then Tom Barton.

The latter made no effort to conceal his resentment. Keith shot a quick look at Mr. Tracy. The manager did not seem to notice the new boy's expression.

Now Mr. Tracy moved to the plate to instruct the young players in bunting. His first words were just what he had announced the previous year—no boy would play until he learned to bunt. He demonstrated the crouch, the level bat, the loose grip. He had them turn completely around in the box, squarely facing the pitcher. Keith wondered what the coach would say about Tom Barton's bunting style. The olive-skinned boy had not shifted his feet at all in tryouts.

The veterans went in for their turns. The machine was set at slow speed; Mr. Tracy believed in making hitting easy at first. If he followed last year's pattern, he would not let them bat against human deliveries for at least a week. Batting, he said, was more confidence than physical ability. The boy who believed he could hit usually did.

Dick's turn first. He was fair with the stick; Keith grinned as his close friend went to the plate with face set in grim lines. What did Dick think about this attention to Abe Duran's catching effort? Dick lashed out three solid blows but looked pitiful bunting.

"Try again, Merrill," Mr. Tracy said coldly. "Just hold the bat still and meet the ball. You have to be smarter than the bat; that is all there is to it."

Tom Barton next with Jacques LeClerc "shagging" off the backstop as Abe took off the pads and Dick hurriedly put them on.

The first delivery—Tom's back foot moved as in tryouts. He met the ball but only weakly.

"Hold it," called out Mr. Tracy to José and Pat, now feeding the machine. He went to the dugout and returned with four bats. "Take your regular stance, Barton," he ordered. The wondering Tom obeyed. The manager carefully spread the bats flat around Tom's rear foot. "Step out again," warned Mr. Tracy, "and you are apt to fall on your face."

"I can't hit this way," Tom protested.

"You won't do any worse," said the manager.

Tom's mouth set in tight lines but he obeyed. His foot still slipped and he hit no ball solid.

"Kick the bats away," said Mr. Tracy, "and try your bunts."

Now comes more trouble, worried Keith, for the Giant manager was stricter about bunting style than anything else. But Mr. Tracy said nothing after Tom had flicked out two rollers in his usual style.

Then the coach called for the attention of every player. "In case you are wondering," he announced, "I like the way Barton bunts. It is really the best way, the big league way. But he is only the second little league player I have ever seen who can do it. Don't any of you try his style."

Tom showed his first smile since practice had started.

"Who taught you to bunt like that, Barton?"

"Nobody. I watch television a lot and that is how Nellie Fox——"

"You picked a good one to imitate," broke in Mr. Tracy. "What did you bat last year in Nashville."

"Not much," Tom confessed. "I pitched mostly and——

"I expect pitchers to hit, too. And you have to play every game, not just six innings a week."

"Yes, sir. I played shortstop——"

"And batted second with pinch hitters coming in for you with runners on base?"

"Yes, sir."

"We will be short of bench strength this year," the manager said tersely. "Too many ten-year-olds. Let's see if you can't develop into a full-time player this year."

Tom hesitated, then mumbled agreement.

Jacques LeClerc batted next. Then Joe Pettus, Dave, Roy, Keith—on through the probable lineup. We will get fairly good hitting, gloated Keith, even without Merle Conroy's home runs in the cleanup position. Pitching, catching, and reserves—solve those worries and the Giants could give any team trouble, even with the loss of last year's stars.

And Mr. Tracy was shortly testing mound prospects—Tom, Joe, Dave, Jacques, even Keith himself. Both mitts were busy as Dick and Abe caught the throws while Mr. Dudley hit fly balls to the other aspirants.

Keith's sidearmed efforts went low, high, wide, anywhere except over the plate. But Mr. Tracy gave quiet encouragement.

"You will do it, Gregg, just like you learned to catch."

Keith wiped sweat from his face. He would try; he promised that.

Another lap, then Keith noticed the waiting taxi. Tom climbed into the rear seat and rode off. How long had the cab been waiting? A half hour anyhow, said Roy Murray. Probably a Cadillac and chauffeur next week, Joe speculated. No walking nor bicycle for Sonny Barton's brother.

"He sure couldn't walk," said Dave Parker. "It's six whole blocks to the Regal Arms."

Keith did his best not to hear such talk. He would only stir up more smart cracks if he took Tom's side. This was little league; the singer's brother must do his own talking. But it took determined effort to keep quiet. What was wrong with these jokers? Didn't they want a winning club? And their chances rode on Tom Barton's pitching arm, that was for sure. Mr. Tracy had assigned the new boy to third but Keith was sure that Tom would start the season at shortstop. Jacques was a sure fielder but could not cover as much ground. A new boy alternating between short and the mound and the best at either position—what did it take to satisfy his new teammates?

Dick walked with him as far as Pecos Street. The towhead was anything but pleased.

"Mr. Dudley acts as if he already has picked Abe to catch," Dick complained.

"I tried to tell you," Keith shrugged. "If you don't get to hustling—well, you can try to make left field."

"I told you once," snapped Dick, "and I'll tell you again. I will be the first string catcher. Abe Duran or nobody else will beat me out. I didn't try so hard last year because you were better than me and I knew it. But Duran—I can catch rings around him."

"Then prove it," said Keith.

He was dead tired when he finally reached home. He settled in a living room chair with a deep sigh. Had last year's first workout been so hard? He didn't think so.

"How did practice go?" asked Mr. Gregg.

"Rough."

"Mr. Tracy hinted that last night. He said his boys would have to go some to stay out of the cellar."

"Well, he wanted ten-year-olds," Keith said with some sourness. The idea of building a future team did not satisfy a boy playing his final season.

"How did young Barton do?"

"He had his troubles," Keith admitted. "Mr. Tracy rode him some." He looked at his father in sudden wonder. "What did Mr. Tracy have to pay for him?"

"That is top secret," said Mr. Gregg. "But it wasn't as much as you think."

"Because he might not play all season?"

"That was the big factor but not the only reason." The players' agent hesitated. "I probably shouldn't say this, but the other managers were a little afraid that Tom might turn out to be more trouble than he is worth. Oh, they bid up the price, sure. But there have been other boys to bring the limit, and he didn't."

Mrs. Gregg had entered the room in time to hear most of this.

"What was Mr. Tracy's attitude?" she wanted to know.

"I think he takes it as a sort of personal challenge," answered Mr. Gregg. "He feels that a big purpose of little league is to deal with young problem personalities."

"Tom isn't that," Keith said quickly. "He is all right, if you just know how to get along with him." He scowled. "I'm real glad Mr. Tracy got him, if that's how the other managers feel."

"So am I," agreed Mrs. Gregg. "I honestly feel sorry for Tom."

"Why?" Keith demanded. "No other boy in this league has so much. You ought to see that apartment and that swimming pool. And there is a taxi waiting to pick him up after practice."

"You are wrong, son," his mother said patiently. "No other boy in the league has so little." A smile came to her face. "We should have known Jim Tracy would take that attitude."

"Sure," Mr. Gregg said gently. "I remember what he said during the auction last year, about a boy whose parents drink too much. He said that if there isn't a heart in little league, then it isn't worth it."

Keith sighed. He wasn't sure that his parents knew what they were talking about. Mr. Tracy had been harder on Tom in this first workout than on any other boy.

CHAPTER 7

O

The Team Takes Shape

Three days of routine practice—batting against the pitching machine, two hitting turns per player, individual infield and outfield tests—Tom complained that this was the dullest practice in his experience.

"We haven't even had a regular infield workout," he grumbled.

"But we're working on fundamentals," Keith said patiently. He had felt the same way in his first season, that the Giants started more slowly than the other teams. "Mr. Tracy coaches us on our regular positions first, then starts getting us to work together."

"You mean he is going to play me at third?"

Keith sighed. It appeared so, and that puzzled him, too. So did the manager's attention to Pat Maguire and Miles Carowe as prospective pitchers. And wasn't Mr. Dudley even going to give Dick a chance at catching? Oh, the towhead was working some behind the plate, for Abe took a regular turn at third base, too. But, if the coaches' concentration meant anything, Duran was already chosen as starting receiver.

"LeClerc should be working at third," went on Tom. "He is okay, just not fast enough. At either third or second, though——"

"Mr. Tracy isn't about to move Jacques, except to pitch him."

"He can't throw anything," Tom snapped.

"He has good control."

"Oh, he can get the ball over the plate." His olive features held their scowl. "Don't we play any practice games? I'm itching to pitch."

"We don't play as many as the other teams," said Keith. "I doubt if we take on anybody before week after next."

Tom sighed. "It doesn't make sense to me. But Sonny says to keep quiet and worry about my own knitting."

"He should have said your own *hitting*," Keith ventured. Sometimes he was annoyed by Tom's attitude, too. He wanted to be the whole show and right now—Dave Parker had said that in the dugout and Keith could not deny it.

"Mr. Tracy is just wasting time," shrugged Tom. "I'll never be a hitter. But I can do enough other things to make up for it. If he'll just put me at shortstop and settle on a pitcher who can get the ball over, we'll win some games. You can hit, and Joe, too, and Roy Murray."

Keith nodded. All three had sent balls out of the park that afternoon. And Dick Merrill had lined one against the wall.

Tom went to the waiting taxi and Keith walked with Dick. More griping, of course. Dick claimed he was throwing better than Abe. Did Mr. Dudley have it in for him? Keith sighed. How could he answer that question? He was far from pleased with practice himself. He still found it awkward to let the mitt sort of dangle on his hand, and Mr. Tracy insisted on that. His sidearmed efforts still went in every direction. And what did their hitting improvement mean as long as they faced the machine? Nearly all of them were getting good wood on the ball, and why not? Every pitch came at the same speed and almost the same height. Even Tom was connecting more solidly, though he protested against Mr. Tracy's recommended stance. He was crouching lower and crowding the plate. When he did connect, he complained, the ball didn't go anywhere.

Defensive drills finally, with Mr. Dudley pitching, Mr. Tracy batting, and seven boys as base runners. And the stern standard Keith recalled from the previous season was still in effect. Safe hits did not count; base runners were held or recalled on them. But let a run score on errors and all eight defensive players circled the field. So did any boy who did not race to his assigned spot at the crack of the bat. There was a place to head on the dead run, a base to back up, a relay or cut-off position to take, either on safe hits, infield rollers, or fly balls.

This exacting drill, Keith knew, would continue all season.

Only two boys received much consideration for these eight defensive positions, Tom at third, and Abe behind the plate. Dick worked as catcher a third of the time, Abe taking third and Tom sitting out. The infield arrangement was different when Tom held the hot corner. Mr. Tracy

had the newcomer playing wider than the usual third
sacker and Jacques LeClerc stationed nearer to second.

There was concentration on the pitcher's fielding, too.
Tom went first, of course, and brought more sharp reprimands from Manager Tracy. He did not like the way Tom
came off the mound. He wanted the pitcher moving with
the throw—to his left on an outside pitch, to the right on
one close to the batter.

"That bothers my follow-through," protested Tom.

He could get used to it, Mr. Tracy pointed out calmly. A
good fielding pitcher was valuable to any team, in Little
League ball especially. Agile hurlers could start as many
double plays as either the shortstop or second baseman.
And especially he must come up for bunts.

The catcher must come out, too. The catcher must call
the throw and call it quick and loud. Neither Abe nor Dick
did that to Mr. Dudley's satisfaction.

"I don't want the pitcher or third baseman even looking
at the runners," explained the ex-college catcher. "So the
catcher has to react quickly and yell it out. We want the
whole infield to hear him."

Abe and Dick took turns again. Mr. Dudley shook his
head after each effort.

"Gregg, come show them how," he said.

Keith was glad to do it. This had not been easy for him
to learn the previous season.

Tom lobbed a pitch to Mr. Dudley; he bunted toward
third base. Runners had been stationed on first and second;
another tore for first. Keith whipped off his mask, ran out,
sized up the situation at a glance.

"Third!" he yelled.

Tom hesitated before throwing, and the lead runner slid in safely.

"Can't you trust your catcher, Barton?" demanded Mr. Tracy.

The olive-skinned boy shook his head. This strategy was new to him, he explained. He had always made such decisions himself.

"I know," nodded the manager. "I've noticed that other leagues don't stress the bunt as much as we do. But it's especially important to you. The better the pitcher, the more he is bunted. Let's try it again with Abe behind the plate."

Dick took the next turn. It seemed to Keith that his friend outdid the new player. In fact, he thought Dick was outdoing Duran in almost every department. The towhead was even shifting his position with every pitch. Keith could not help grinning as he went back to first base. Dick could not be charged with indifferent effort these afternoons. His throwing, hitting, even his base-running—there was no doubting his determination to recover what he had taken for granted, the regular catching assignment.

Defensive drill—golly, how many afternoons would Mr. Tracy concentrate on that? And with the drill came the laps, often on Keith's wild throws.

"If we are run to death," panted Joe Pettus, "it'll be your fault, Gregg."

Pitching miscues brought almost as much punishment. Pat Maguire had trouble coming off the mound, too, as did Roy Murray. But neither had pitched before, at least not in the major league, and Mr. Tracy was patient with them. But not with Tom Barton. He threw wild and to the wrong base and a runner scored. Mr. Tracy stopped the disgusted start on another lap.

"Just Barton," the manager said curtly. "No reason to run the rest of you ragged because he won't learn."

Tom voiced no complaint but there was no misunderstanding his expression. Keith sighed. If this kept up, maybe Tom would decide it had been a mistake to establish residence in West Austin. "Riding" Tom, ignoring Dick—and Keith had both to comfort. Separately, of course, for his two friends seemed to avoid each other. Tom was that way with all other teammates, however. If his attitude was softening at all, Keith could not tell it.

It was something to worry about, he brooded as he left Dick at Pecos Street and walked home alone. Weren't managers supposed to treat every boy alike? Well, Mr. Tracy certainly didn't. The manager never spoke to Keith except in quiet encouragement. He was taking daily turns as a pitcher, despite his wildness. Mr. Tracy worked him at fielding off the mound, too, shifting Roy to first base. Murray showed a knack for handling the bag, too; Keith would not complain if Mr. Tracy decided to start Murray at the position. And Pat Maguire—the manager hovered like a mother hen over this ten-year-old pitching prospect. Was Pat worth so much attention? He was a slight, bespectacled boy who had learned to throw a roundhouse curve in the minor league. His efforts at a fast ball Keith was willing to catch barehanded. But, if these practice sessions meant anything, Mr. Tracy intended to use Pat on the mound this year.

Of course, there wasn't much choice—Keith had to admit that. This team was nothing like the championship outfit of the previous season. The Giants could expect to win some games, yes, when Tom pitched. Both Dick and Abe grabbed the sponge when catching Tom's practice throws.

But the rest of the team showed little. Even he, Joe, Dave, and the other returning regulars were failing to show last year's form. And the other teams were said to be stronger. The Dodgers had already beaten the Reds in a practice contest. Winston and Calumet had a game scheduled the next day. Three teams were almost ready for the season, and Atlas was actually not even started!

Mr. Gregg had watched part of the practice; he usually did. He looked up from his newspaper as Keith came glumly into the house.

"Why are you so down and out?"

Keith sighed. Practice, he confessed. They were not doing any good.

"I would agree," nodded his father, "except for one thing."

What was that? What encouraging sign had Mr. Gregg observed?

"I sat by Don Thomas a while," his father said. "This is his third year as president and his eighth season of following the league closely. Several of us talked about how ragged you are looking and he just laughed. He said he had heard the same story every season. All through April practices, the parents stew and fuss about sloppy Giant practices. The league followers count Jim Tracy's team out every April, he said, and then are shocked when Atlas wins the season's opener. And your team has done that every year but one."

Keith sighed again. He knew that. Only Winston had ever beaten Atlas in an opening game; that was year before last when the Reds had won their only championship.

"You have two weeks to go," Mr. Gregg pointed out.

Keith nodded. Just two weeks. And who was ready to play a regulation game? The infield, maybe. And not many outfield worries either, not unless one of the three returning twelve-year-olds was sick or injured. Dave, Roy, and Davis Gordon had proved their abilities last year. But pitching, catching, hitting! "We just aren't organized," Keith worried. "And we don't have any pitching except for Tom."

"Why are you so modest all of a sudden? I understand sidearm pitches worry Little League hitters. And you are sure throwing hard enough."

"Gosh, I won't pitch any," Keith protested. "I'll be lucky to hold first base."

The telephone rang.

"Answer it, please," Mrs. Gregg called from the kitchen.

Keith obeyed. "Ah would like to talk to your mother, Keith," said the voice at the other end of the line. There was no mistaking that drawl.

Keith called his mother. "Sonny Barton wants to talk to you," he said.

"Sonny? What in the world about?"

The telephone was in the den; Keith and his father heard every word she said.

"Yes, Sonny?——Why, I suppose so, but—certainly, Sonny, come right out. I'll be happy to talk to you."

"Now what?" asked Mr. Gregg as she put down the

telephone. "I thought young Barton's financial empire was my exclusive worry."

"I have no idea," she said. "He wants my advice on something of a personal nature. He is coming out."

"Do I have to worry about him at home, too?" asked Mr. Gregg with a sigh. "His business takes up half my mornings, what with his records and the various commissions he has to pay and duplicate deposit slips for his Nashville accountants."

"Is his business doing all right? Locating in Austin hasn't hurt him?"

"In some ways," answered the lawyer. "There are some additional costs. For instance, he has legal counsel on retainer in Nashville, too. He has to keep driving to have anything left for himself."

"Well, dinner is ready," Mrs. Gregg announced, "and I know you two are hungry."

Keith did not have to be persuaded. He was nearly starved.

The doorbell rang before they had finished eating. Mr. Gregg started to rise; his wife stopped him.

Neither Keith nor his father ventured into the living room. They heard the faint hum of voices, but could not make any of the actual conversation out. Father and son moved from the dining table to chairs before the television set.

Mrs. Gregg rejoined them within a few minutes. Sonny had departed, she said, declining to join them.

"What was it all about?" Mr. Gregg asked curiously.

"You won't breathe a word of it?"

"I promise on my Southern honor," he said gravely.

"How about you, Keith? You won't tell any of your friends?"

The boy hesitated, then nodded. What sort of secret could his mother and Sonny Barton be sharing?

"It floored me momentarily," Mrs. Gregg said after a sort of gasp. "The famous Sonny Barton wants a date with Barbee Brush."

Mr. Gregg smiled and reached for his pipe. "Does that come under our jurisdiction?" he asked. "I've been congratulating myself all these years that I don't have a daughter to worry about."

"Don't treat it as a joke. It's not the usual thing."

"It sure wouldn't be if she were my daughter," agreed Mr. Gregg.

"Of course not. That is why he came to me for help. He knows that Barbee's parents are going to frown on the idea."

"I suppose you are going to represent him, be a feminine version of John Alden?"

"No," Mrs. Gregg said firmly. "But I advised him to get out of his flashy costumes, leave his special car at the hotel, and use either a rented car or a taxi, and politely ask permission of her parents to take her to a picture show."

The lawyer hesitated. "In other words, step completely out of character? That's sound counsel," agreed Mr. Gregg. He regarded his wife with twinkling eyes. "But, even so, what would you do if you were Barbee's mother?"

"I don't know," she confessed. "I am sympathetic with him, of course. I have seen the other side of him."

"When?"

"When he sang that folk song, that lullaby."

The lawyer smiled. "Quite obviously he won you over with that. Or perhaps it was the dedication. He is singing more of that type of song, by the way, or did I tell you?"

"You told me."

"He even made a record of 'Turn Around,' or whatever the song is called," Mr. Gregg went on. "But his distributors shipped it right back with the strong warning that such a release might ruin him." Mr. Gregg shook his head. "He is in too deep a rut to change, professionally or socially. I rather pity him myself, as much as I can grieve for any seventeen-year-old boy already worth half a million dollars."

"That much?"

"He could shut down and end up with about that." He puffed his pipe. "Keep me posted about further developments. I'm curious to know how Tom Brush reacts to this crisis. He appreciates rock-and-roll about as much as I do."

"I will," Mrs. Gregg promised. She turned to Keith. "Now remember, young man," she said severely, "not a word of this to any of your friends."

Keith shrugged his shoulders. He was worried about Little League baseball, not about who had dates with Barbee Brush.

CHAPTER 8

O

The Giants Show Muscle

Keith had mixed feelings about the practice game with the Reds. Tom Barton would prove his pitching ability; Keith looked forward to watching the Giant ace handle such hitters as Tobe Wingo, Dan Poggin, and Doyle Chandler. But Tom would pitch only two innings, probably, and then what? And how would Atlas hitters fare against Dan and Seth Mitchell? All other teams boasted at least two experienced hurlers. The Cats had three—Ruel, Louis Chastain, and Mike Levy. The latter's showing in practice contests was a surprise. Doyle claimed that he was faster even than Ruel.

But Tom, insisted Keith, would overshadow all rivals. Unless their defense cracked up, the Giants could best any opponent with Barton on the mound.

"Pitchers don't win ball games by themselves," scoffed Ruel. "He might have been big game in that Tennessee league but he is just animal crackers to us."

Mr. Tracy's starting lineup was no surprise to Keith,

except for Abe Duran as catcher. He looked to Dick to see how the towhead reacted and saw what he had expected, anger and resentment. Keith sighed and led the Giants out of the dugout when the volunteer umpire signaled to play ball. Was Dick right? Was he a victim of Mr. Dudley's personal feeling?

Tom walked slowly to the mound. Quite a few spectators sat in the stands, more than the usual number to watch a practice game. Keith could guess why—they were curious about the newcomer's ability.

Tom wasted no time impressing them. He struck out Duke Canfield with four pitches, all fast balls. Abe whipped the ball to Keith and it went on around the diamond before getting back to the hurler. David Baker missed a curve by a foot, then swung vainly at two high pitches. Keith grinned in appreciation of Tom's strategy. Buffalo a batter, get him swinging, then throw high ones!

Doyle Chandler now. Keith retreated to the edge of the grass. Now, he mused, they would find out just how good a pitcher Tom was. Doyle had led the league in home runs as an eleven-year-old, starting on the all-star team. He would surely repeat as a first baseman, too, Keith thought ruefully. There was no hope of his improving enough to beat Doyle out.

This left-handed hitter stood deep in the box but he was not a setup for a curve; Keith remembered that from the previous season. Doyle had driven one of Merle's prize curves over the right field fence to break up a close contest.

Keith saw Tom take a deep breath. The pitcher sensed the test; maybe he had heard of Doyle's plate prowess from other boys. Tom shook off the first signal. He threw his fast-breaking pitch low and on the outside corner. Doyle cut and missed. The ball got away from Abe, too; the Giant catcher chased it back to the wire. This pitcher would not be easy to hold, thought Keith.

Now a fast one, letter high. Doyle fouled it off, swinging late. Golly, chortled Keith. Doyle was a puller, but he had sure hit behind this offering. The batter stepped out of the box, rubbed his hands in the dirt, set his feet again. Another signal refused. A second. Keith tensed. One finger was a fast ball, two a curve. What could the other signal be—let up or crossfire?

It was the latter. Doyle let it pass and stalked away immediately, confirming the umpire's decision.

Golly, golly, gloated Keith. Three batters faced, three strikeouts. If they had two Tom Bartons, they would have this league in their hands.

Jacques led off. He worked Dan to a two-two count before fishing at a low, wide curve. Tom stepped into the box. He was a weak hitter, all right, but he didn't advertise that fact. He faced Dan as if confident of his plate ability. The first pitch was a called strike. The second——

His bunt caught the Crimson infield by surprise. There was no hint of his intention, just a dribble between pitcher and first base. Poggin hurried but Tom easily beat the throw. Gosh, thought Keith, Tom could bunt two hundred!

Down streaked the runner on the first pitch. Mr. Tracy hadn't called a steal; Joe had hit away. But he missed Dan's fast ball and Tobe's throw was too slow. Tom slid into the base without any effort at a tag by Steve Kalumus.

A hit means a run—more than one voice reminded Joe of

that. The second baseman choked his bat slightly and leaned closer to the plate. Ball one. Strike two. Then Joe lifted a humpbacked liner over second base. Tom rounded third at full speed and stormed into home. He might have been out if Ronny Bellamy had thrown a hard strike, but not with the peg wide by two steps. Joe took second standing up.

It was Keith's turn now. He let one pass, then slapped a single behind the runner. The ball was just out of Steve's reach; Joe scored.

Dave and Roy struck out but Keith's eyes danced as he took throws from his fellow infielders while Tom threw his warm-ups. Just like that—two runs off Dan Poggin! Three base hits, too, earned tallies all.

Maybe his team was better than he had thought. He looked for his father in the stands. There Mr. Gregg sat with Mr. Thomas. Keith grunted, remembering the words of the president repeated to him. The same talk every April, he had said—how ragged the Giants looked. But, with the season's opener a week off, it was Atlas 2, Winston 0.

And three more strikeouts by grim Tom Barton! What a start in this league, chortled Keith.

Dan set down three straight batters. Bespectacled Pat Maguire came out to pitch for the Giants with Tom replacing Joe Weiman at third base. Now, sighed Keith, the Atlas defense must get to work. Anybody could get wood on Pat's slow offerings.

Tobe Wingo hit the first pitch, a solid slash toward left. It would have been a base hit except for Tom Barton's position; the third sacker was wide of the bag and deeper than Keith had ever seen a hot-corner man play. Tom knocked down the bouncing ball, scooped it up and threw hurriedly.

His peg was wide but Keith reacted instinctively. He left the base, speared the ball one-handed and tagged out the runner.

He grinned at Mr. Tracy's praise from the dugout. Maybe he would learn to use this pad after all.

This time Keith remembered to observe Tom's position before the pitch. He crouched wide of the base, still deep. LeClerc was almost to second base. Ron Bellamy hit one through the box but Jacques trapped it and Ron was an easy out.

Duke Canfield singled but Roy retired the Reds with a running catch in right center. Still 2–0, exulted Keith. Young Pat could be hit, sure, but he had stout backing, especially with Tom playing such an unconventional third base.

They got a third run off Seth Mitchell. Then Pat Maguire served up more of his roundhouses, giving Winston their first run on a double and two singles. But the over-shifted Atlas defense turned another well-hit ball into a double play. Jacques took a grounder past the pitcher, stepped on second and threw to first.

"Warm up, Keith," Mr. Tracy said as the Giants came in for their turn at bat.

"Me!" Keith could hardly believe his own ears.

The manager nodded and Dick said gruffly, "Come on." Keith grunted and followed the towhead to the bullpen behind the fence.

He threw rapidly; Seth was wasting no time with the

Giant hitters. Then he trudged toward the mound as Dick donned the catcher's gear and Roy took first base. Other lineup changes sent Abe to third and Miles, José, and Tim into the outfield.

Keith sighed. He must worry not only about his own control but also about his defensive backing.

Both failed him. He walked the first three batters. Then he marked up a strikeout; one of Winston's new players swung at a wide offering. Tobe lifted a high deep fly to center field. Probably Roy would have caught it against the fence, but ten-year-old Miles faltered. Two runs scored. The usually dependable Jacques fumbled a fairly easy grounder.

Keith looked hopefully to Mr. Tracy but the manager did not stir. Gritting his teeth, Keith faced Dan Poggin. What should he do, throw and duck? Dan usually powdered the ball and there were two runners on.

Dan swung and missed the first pitch. A second pitch was over; Dan fouled it off. Keith licked his dry lips and decided to try a let-up, a "palm ball" such as Tom threw.

It worked. Dan lifted an easy foul effort for Abe to gather in.

But then came two more walks, forcing a run across the plate. Duke smashed the first pitch right back at Keith. He speared it neatly but this was small consolation for him. He had sloughed off the Giant lead. He gestured helplessly to Mr. Tracy as he went into the dugout.

"Shrug it off," said the manager with a faint smile.

Keith sighed. How could he? Atlas must come up with more pitchers, all right—Tom could pitch only six innings a week. But Mr. Tracy might as well scrap any notion that Keith Gregg could become that pitching reinforcement.

The Giants scored again. Dick marched to the plate with fire in his eyes and slammed one against the center-field boards. He moved to third on Tim's bunt and scored on a passed ball. Keith grinned approvingly. Now Dick was even running bases as if he meant business.

Back to the mound for Keith; Mr. Tracy gestured that and Keith did not protest, not aloud anyway. He threw as well as he could and just shut his eyes when one Crimson batter after another trotted to first base after the fourth ball.

Finally Winston was retired, after four more runs. Keith went slowly to the dugout. He watched glumly as the three Giant ten-year-olds went out in order.

It was Winston's game. Keith's lips twitched. He did not mind the loss so much; he knew how Mr. Tracy felt about these warm-up games. Atlas's first victory the year before had come in the opening doubleheader, not in a practice contest. Mr. Tracy almost seemed to make sure that his players lost the games which did not count in the league standings.

But his miserable pitching efforts—Keith could not shrug that off. Tears welled in his eyes as he bent over the water fountain. He drank his fill, then turned to Tom Barton.

"Nice work," he said gruffly. "You showed them what they can expect all season."

Tom's olive features showed no elation. "I wish you could have done better," he said huskily. "Mr. Tracy should have pulled you."

"I will decide about that, Barton," said a familiar voice behind them. Mr. Tracy was standing right beside them.

"Yes, sir," muttered Tom. He hesitated, then added, unable to conceal his feeling, "But I hated to see Keith suffer like that. He was doing his best. He just can't——"

"Get the ball over," the manager agreed. His hand fell lightly on Tom's shoulder. "I appreciate your attitude, Tom," he added, speaking gently, to Keith's surprise. He had expected his friend to catch the dickens for daring to criticize Mr. Tracy's strategy. "Keith has proved a stout friend and you should take up for him at the drop of a hat. But I know what I'm doing; at least I *think* I do."

The manager's other hand gripped Keith's elbow. "This boy may get back the full use of his arm," said Mr. Tracy, "and he may not. I hope he does. When he can whip the ball overhanded, he can go back to catching. But I have to develop him into a ball player even if he must throw side-armed the rest of his life. He is wild now, sure, much too wild. But I know Keith. He will improve his control all along. And that motion of his—sort of jerky—he gets a wrinkle without trying."

Tom considered this an instant, then nodded. "They didn't really hit him—except when he had to ease up."

But Keith was only partially satisfied by the coach's explanation. Wasn't Mr. Tracy putting consideration for one boy ahead of the team? He mentioned this to his father, who asked for details, then chuckled softly.

"You should be grateful for that attitude."

"I am," Keith said quickly. "But I want us to win again. All we need is a pitcher to back up Tom and——"

"I wouldn't say that," the players' agent disagreed

mildly. "Nor would I say that Jim Tracy isn't out to win just as much as you are. He doesn't have many prospects to choose from. Young Pat Maguire, yes, for short stints. But who else?"

"Jacques LeClerc or Joe Pettus."

"That would tear up a good infield"

"Tom could play short and Abe take care of third. Dick can outcatch Abe anyhow."

"Sure, when he decides to do it." The lawyer smiled. "And he acted today as if he intends to do just that."

Games against the Dodgers and the Cats followed the same pattern of defeat for Atlas. Tom was invincible in his turn, Pat consistent and unruffled by opposing bats, then Keith wild and ineffective. Dave Parker worked one inning against Calumet and showed calmness under pressure, if nothing else. The Cats tagged him for a score but good defensive support stopped further damage.

But one lineup change sent Keith home almost as happy as if he had made a good showing himself.

"Merrill," Mr. Tracy asked suddenly, as the Giants sat in the dugout while the Cats held their infield drill, "are you ready to start catching?'

"I sure am," the towhead shot back.

The manager studied Dick doubtfully. "Then we'll try it," he said calmly. "But don't let up, not for one minute. I don't like to alternate catchers. It will be either your job or Abe's, and I can depend on him to do his best."

"Me, too," Dick promised.

And he had kept his word through the five innings he caught. Abe relieved him, then, but not because of any lapse in performance. All boys played in these practice games, a fact which made them even harder to judge by regular-season standards. The "grapefruit" schedule, spring exhibition games, meant nothing in major league baseball; Keith read the sports pages enough to realize that. The New York Yankees, for instance, were well down in the exhibition standings, but still solid favorites to repeat as American League champions.

And the Giants were the Yankees of West Austin, the team to beat every year.

The early schedule favored them, gloated Keith. A Saturday doubleheader opened the league, then Winston met Bedford Monday with the Giants facing Calumet on Tuesday. Tom could pitch all of the first two games; Little League rules required a full seventy-two hour rest for any hurler used more than three innings. That would get Atlas off to a 2–0 start, with a full game lead over the field. The other teams would be playing catch-up after the third game.

He was stretched out on his bed with that dream; his mother interrupted. The Cactus Pryor show was featuring Sonny Barton, she announced. Didn't Keith want to see it?

It didn't matter much to him, but he did join his mother and father in the den. The image on the screen was different, he realized after a moment. Sonny had put aside his showy costumes for a sports shirt and slacks—he looked like any high school boy except for his long sideburns.

"You are watching a fairly shrewd propaganda campaign," Mr. Gregg explained dryly.

What did his father mean? The lawyer showed a faint

smile. "Sonny did not get his date with his next-door neighbor. Barbee's father ruled against him as a cheap exhibitionist—those are Mr. Brush's exact words. But our young friend doesn't give up easily. This program is meant to convince him—and perhaps other narrow-minded fathers in West Austin—that Sonny Barton is the typical All-American boy when he's not after folding money."

Keith smiled, too. He did not understand every word his father said; he seldom did. But he had learned to grasp what his father meant.

"He's using just ballads," added Mr. Gregg. "A singer's night off—that's what he calls this program. Meet the real boy behind the glitter and tinsel and specially built convertible."

"Don't be sarcastic," said Keith's mother. "Why shouldn't he want nice company sometimes, nice girls his own age?"

"Oh, I am all for the boy," Mr. Gregg said quickly. "He is my client and a good one. And I am loyal to my clients."

Keith was not sure that he understood just what this was all about. It seemed to him that Tom's brother was going to a lot of trouble for very little reason. Surely he had met better looking girls than Barbee. Luke Doyle's older sister, for instance. Jeanie was more fun, too. Sometimes she wrestled Luke to the floor and tickled his ribs until he begged for mercy. Jeanie would take so much teasing and no more.

CHAPTER 9

O

You Can't Do It All, Son!

Atlas was the home team. Another break, thought Keith; he always felt better about a game when his side would get last bat. He sat on the dugout steps and watched the Reds take their infield drill. The Winston starter had already been announced, Dan Poggin. Tom would go for the Giants, of course; the olive-skinned boy was throwing to Dick outside the fence.

Just seconds remained now until the opening ceremony. Mr. Thomas stood waiting with portable microphone to introduce the honor battery. The color guard was ready for the march to the flagpole in center field. Keith shivered and rechecked his shoelaces. He was almost as nervous as he had been the previous year, when all this had been brand new, when he had been doubtful of his ability to jump from the minors to starting catcher. Now, at least, he had confidence in his hitting and fielding; he had learned to handle first base well enough. Oh, he was no Doyle Chandler, but who else was in this league? The Giants gave up nothing at first base to either the Dodgers or the Cats, the teams expected to finish one-two.

As for the other two, the pre-season guessers gave the Crimson credit for good hitting, though spotty, and fair pitching, but pointed out their weakness in the outfield. The Giants had all-around strength except for substitutes, but lacked a second pitcher and expected to lose Tom Barton before the season ended.

Keith sighed. He could not dispute that general size-up of this season's prospects, except that——

Well, Mr. Tracy had said it for him just moments before.

"Don't let what you hear worry you," he had told his players. "Just keep thinking about one thing. We'll hold the championship until some team takes it away from us."

There would be no start toward that today, Keith thought happily, not with Tom Barton going the full route.

The brief speeches finally started. Then came the flag-raising, a scratchy recording of "The Star-Spangled Banner," and the umpires coming through the left field gate——

"Play ball!"

Out charged the Giant starters with shrill, defiant yells, except for the pitcher, of course. Tom walked slowly to the mound, head down, his right hand flapping against his thigh. He threw three fast balls, then warned Dick of his curve. The pitch broke sharply and the catcher could not hold it. Keith frowned. Passed balls would plague the Giants regularly until Dick learned to hold Tom's breaking stuff. That was no reflection on the towhead's ability either; probably no receiver in the league could do better. Keith Gregg could, perhaps. He had handled Merle Conroy, the league's top hurler of last season. But Keith was at first base, maybe never to don catching regalia again.

But batters couldn't get first base on a missed third strike—the blessing of that Little League concession came with the first batter. Steve Kalumas took two blazing fast balls, then missed a dropping curve. The pitch got away from Dick and went all the way to the wire, but Steve was out automatically.

Eddie Wilson was a "K," too, after one foul tip. Dan Poggin now; the Giant defense moved deeper out of respect for the hitter. But Dan fared no better than his two Crimson predecessors. Three batters, three strikeouts! Tom showed no emotion at all as he went to the bench. His expression suggested that he had expected nothing else, and that five more innings of the same were coming up.

And maybe they were, thought Keith. How many fair balls had been hit off Tom in practice games? Very few indeed. The defense had just stood around and watched him retire batters single-handed.

They needed a run—Keith led that chorus. They had hit Poggin before and they could again.

But not in this frame, except for Joe's scratch single. Keith made the last out himself, lifting a rainmaker to right field. But the Giants were getting wood at least, he comforted himself.

The Reds couldn't make that claim. Doyle Chandler tipped two, then went out on a fast, letter-high pitch. Probably he was set for a curve, thought Keith, certainly not one right down the middle at his favorite height. Tobe Wingo, the rather bowlegged but capable catcher, missed a streaking fast one. Then Tom gave him the let-up, the "palm" pitch Keith was struggling to master. Wingo let it pass for a second called strike. Then Tom tried two high pitches, but the veteran catcher refused to bite. But the sharp-breaking curve got him. Two away, the strength of Winston's batting order subdued completely. The next four hitters were horse-collar boys, the reasons for not rating the Reds as title threats. Seth Mitchell took all the way, five pitchers. Tom walked to the dugout with his strikeout string unbroken.

Mr. Tracy was waiting for him. "Pace yourself, Barton," cautioned the manager. "You're putting everything you have into every pitch."

"I'm just getting warmed up," said Tom with a shrug.

He's right, thought Keith, grabbing a helmet to coach at first base. Tom Barton seemed blessed with a rubber arm. Keith had never seen a boy who threw more smoothly.

Dave led off with a single. Roy bunted the second pitch and Parker took second. Duck on the pond, Keith yelled to Davis Gordon. A sharp grounder to second let Dave move on to third. But he died there despite Dick's grim effort. The towhead's drive was speared by shortstop Eddie Wilson, and another goose egg went up on the scoreboard.

Keith took it upon himself to repeat Mr. Tracy's warning as Tom finished his warm-up. Keith gestured for the ball and Dick lobbed it to him.

"Three mullets coming up," he told Tom. "They'll be taking. You can take it easy this inning."

The pitcher said nothing but a flash of his dark eyes was answer enough. He was pitching this game and he was doing it very well indeed.

Duke Canfield led off for Winston, and he was taking

just as Keith had predicted. The Reds called encouragement and advice from the dugout. "Don't help him, Duke. Make it be in there."

Ball one. Ball two. Keith saw the scowl on Tom's face. The pitch had been close, all right, certainly no more than an inch off the outside corner. Duke was crowding the plate, the usual strategy when a team meant to "wait out" a pitcher. Keith rubbed some dust in his hands and echoed several calls to Tom to take his time. The first three Crimson hitters would give him little trouble if he just threw strikes.

Did Tom know how to ease up? He had never showed this ability, but it hadn't been necessary before. If he even tried to, Keith could not tell it. On each pitch he went through the same stretch and sweeping motion—hard, blazing throws.

But each one was over, right over, one right behind the other. And strike three! He had thrown neither curve nor letup, but still had plenty of stuff on every pitch.

Dave Baker, nervous but determined, stood in tight, grip shortened. Ball, strike, ball, two more strikes, and he walked back to the dugout, shaking his head.

The voice of Mr. Thomas came over the public address system; he usually announced the games in addition to serving as league president.

"Ladies and gentlemen, Tom Barton of the Giants has just set a league record for consecutive strikeouts in one game."

Spectators in both sections of the grandstand, along the fences and in parked automobiles joined in the applause. Keith's lips twitched. What a way to start the season, especially in a league debut! He had been dead right; Tom Barton would break all West Austin pitching records. Why had he worried even for an instant? This graceful, swarthy boy had this game completely in hand. You only had to look at him to know that. His control going—nuts! He had not walked a batter yet—still another league record was surely being challenged there.

Strike. Ball. Strike. Strike three!

Keith ran to grab Tom's shoulder. "I knew you could do it," he chortled.

The pitcher had no answer.

"Now some runs," whooped Joe Pettus. "Let's get something on the scoreboard."

And they did. Abe Duran justified Mr. Tracy's judgment by singling through the box. Keith, coaching at first, had to concede that he had not realized Abe's potential value to the team. A boy who could play outfield, third base, come in to catch, and also deliver at the plate—no wonder Mr. Tracy had wanted him.

The sacrifice sign was on for Jacques LeClerc, for the first pitch. The shortstop stabbed and missed a low offering, but Keith sent Abe down anyway. For catcher Wingo juggled the bouncing ball and then couldn't find the handle! When he finally did, it was too late to throw.

The bunt was still on; Keith relayed the signal to Abe. This time Jacques met the ball. His trickler was an easy out, Dan to first base, but Duran took third.

Tom Barton was up now, applauded from all directions as he stepped into the box. The hand clapping bothered him not at all. How could he hold such a poker face, wondered Keith. Surely he had never fanned the first nine batters before.

Would he hit away? Keith watched Mr. Tracy. The manager made three meaningless gestures, then touched his cap twice. Tom would bunt, all right, but Abe was to wait for the throw to first before streaking home. The call was for the second pitch; the batter would take the first offering. It came in high for a ball. Tom made no gesture to shift his feet, but then he wouldn't, not until the last instant. The infield was in close but not at bunt depth.

Dan touched the resin bag, toed the rubber, then threw carefully. There it came, a slow, twisting drag between pitcher and first baseman. Neither could reach it easily and Abe Duran showed the quick reaction of a natural player. Instead of waiting for a play at first, Abe charged home. Both runners were safe.

One away. Tom's sudden move took Keith by surprise. There was no signal from the dugout and no word from his base coach—his bid for second was his own idea. He was out by a full step, too, and then Joe lifted a pop-up to retire the side.

Keith, hurrying to the dugout, heard Mr. Tracy's words to the pitcher.

"It isn't up to you to decide when to go, Barton. We had our best hitters coming up. You may have cost us a run or two."

"I thought I could make it," Tom muttered.

He was scowling as he went to the mound. Keith could guess what the pitcher was thinking. He had struck out nine batters and driven in the first run, but his coach criticized his base running!

Keith sighed and rolled the infield practice ball into the dugout. He remembered his father's remark—Tom Barton would not be an easy boy to manage.

Steve Kalumas broke the strikeout string with an easy roller to Keith. Neither did Eddie get solid wood on the ball with his pop-up to Jac. Dan Poggin was the first Crimson hitter to meet a pitch solidly; his line drive curved foul down the right field line. It would have been in for extra bases if fair; Keith sighed in relief. Tom had set one strike-out record; now Keith wanted the swarthy boy to get a no-hitter. Was Tom thinking about that? Surely so, for he was only seven outs away from it.

Tom tried a curve and it broke low and outside. Now the pitcher shook off a signal. He threw another breaking ball, wide and high. Then his letup came in wide, too. Three-one. Keith knew that Dick would call for the fast one; Mr. Tracy did not believe in curves on three-one counts. So it was, off the corner, too. Dan trotted to first.

The perfect game was gone, and a Winston runner on. And at the plate was Doyle Chandler. Tom refused another signal. His curve broke in for a called strike. Doyle would be swinging now, thought Keith, and Tom had better pitch carefully. What if there were two out? This rangy Crimson first baseman could change the game's tide with one swing. Don't give him anything good, Tom. Better to let him take first than connect solidly.

Tom Barton seemed to feel the same way. He threw three straight balls and refused Dick's first call on three-one. The "palm" ball was off center and Doyle took first base.

Still two away, chattered Keith and his teammates. No worry yet, Tommy boy.

But a walk to Tobe Wingo changed that—the third consecutive base on balls. Out came Mr. Tracy to talk to his pitcher. Keith ran to the mound.

"I'm all right," Tom told his manager. "I can get the fast one over, all right. I just wasn't taking any chances."

Mr. Tracy seemed satisfied. "Sure," he said assuringly. "You're past the trouble now. Just get it over. And take more time about it."

Tom nodded. Keith slowly returned to his position. Seth Mitchell was only a so-so hitter. If Tom recovered his control——

Tom proved what he had told his manager, that he could blaze the ball right over. One effort was high and inside, but the other three split the plate and Seth was out swinging. Ten strikeouts in four innings, gloated Tom. What was the league record for total strikeouts in one game?

More runs, insurance—Keith grabbed his favorite bat and went to the plate in time to that chant. And he hit cleanly. Dan's second offering streaked into left center for a long single. Dave moved him to second. Roy hit cleanly to left. Keith might have made home but his third base coach held palms down; he pulled up. Roy took second unchallenged. Two ducks on, Davis Gordon drew a base on balls, and the sacks were jammed.

Dick strode to the plate determined, very determined. He let a ball pass, then flied to center. Keith had checked up carefully; his coach yelled for him to go. He ran with all he had and slid hard, but Ron Bellamy's throw was right on the money. Two out.

Then three as Abe Duran fanned.

But the Giants' one-run lead looked bigger every minute, especially as Tom showed the same accuracy with his fast ball.

There were tips, one line foul to right, a roller outside first base, but Canfield, Baker, and Bellamy went down cutting. Thirteen strikeouts now, still a no-hitter working. Keith edged up to Mr. Tracy to ask about the league record for a full game.

"He just tied it," the manager said tersely. "If he doesn't give out——"

He left the sentence unfinished. Keith yielded the first base coaching spot to Joe Weiman and waited his turn in the circle. He might get up this inning with Jac leading off. If so, it would be with men on base——

He did get up. Jac worked Dan for a walk. Tom fluffed two bunt efforts, then struck out, but Joe cracked a single to center. Jac held. Keith, leaning in, lips tight, met Dan's second pitch squarely. The ball streaked to right center. Both runners went and Keith——

He pulled up with a groan. For Bellamy stabbed that smash one-handed and held on to it even as he slid to his knees. And the quick throw to second doubled off Jac.

Keith stood still, hardly believing what he had seen, then slowly went to get his mitt. He met Tom as the pitcher started for the mound.

"You hit it center," Tom comforted him. "You can't do anything about catches like that."

He surely couldn't, Keith sighed. Two runs would have given the Giants a good lead; now they faced the top of the sixth only one tally to the good, and Steve Kalumas up for Winston.

Now it was plain to see that Tom was tiring. Steve pulled a foul into left field, the first Crimson to swing ahead of the pitch. Tom was bothered and showed it. He rejected Dick's signal in favor of a curve. It was wide. Another ball. A called strike—golly, thought Keith, the Reds were still taking! But why shouldn't they, with the pitcher taking more and more time, his strain there for all to watch. Keith saw Pat Maguire and José Aguirre leave the dugout. His lips twitched. Just three more outs, Tom boy, he whispered.

Then two! For Steve swung desperately at a curve and Mr. Thomas's announcement caused Keith to break out in goose bumps.

"Ladies and gentlemen, Tom Barton has just set a new record for strikeouts in a single game."

Eddie Wilson stood right on the plate, bat choked. Tom rubbed resin on his fingers, toed the rubber, sent up his palm ball.

Eddie met it squarely. Keith's heart skipped a beat until he saw that Roy could reach the ball. The center-fielder must take it deep, backed against the fence. But hitting to Roy was putting it in the well for sure, and there were two away.

"One more out and let's go home," Keith told Tom, handing the ball to the pitcher.

Tom nodded and tried to grin. He studied Dan an instant, then went to the resin bag again. He depended on his curves, as if knowing that the zip was gone from his fast ball. His three-two effort was low and inside; Dan trotted to first.

Doyle Chandler! Out came Mr. Tracy again; Joe and Keith met him at the mound.

"Put him on?" Keith asked anxiously.

"I think not," the manager said. "That would be putting the go-ahead run on. Can you handle one more, Tom?"

Tom nodded, lips tight.

But he was wrong, dead wrong. Doyle sliced the second curve, but with enough behind the bat, with enough height —his curving line drive barely cleared the left center fence, but inches were enough. Keith kicked at the bag at first. Now they were behind 2–1. Joe ran up to the box. We still have our half of the inning, he told the weary pitcher.

Tom waved Joe away and threw like a wild man. Speed, nothing but speed. Ball one, ball two. Then strike one, strike two. Another hard one came in, Wingo swung, and the side was out. That made the strikeout record even more impressive. But Winston led 2–1 and the Reds held that lead. Tom Barton's record went for nothing.

"Too bad, son," Mr. Tracy told the defeated pitcher, "but shake it off. You can learn to pace yourself, and that's all you need."

Tom did not look up. He was having to bite his lips to keep from crying. He succeeded better than Keith, whose eyes were still wet when he climbed into the back seat of the car. They had lost with Tom Barton on the mound! He had not even considered that shattering prospect. He leaned back against the cushions and shut his eyes. If he was brokenhearted, then how must Tom feel! One out away from a no-hitter and a shutout, then wham! One clean lick and both dreams exploded!

○

CHAPTER 10

The Giants Regroup

The Dodgers had won over Calumet in the opening doubleheader; the Cats turned around Monday and nosed out the Reds 5–4. Let Tom Barton post his first victory and the league standings would be all even.

But Bedford's ace could go the full route, too, and Rene Ramirez was every bit as effective as Dan Poggin. The Giants must pull on their hitting breeches, Keith mused grimly. Their first defeat was more the team's failure than Tom's personal shortcoming. They had backed him up with only one run. They had connected with Dan's offerings, but hadn't bunched their hits. Give Tom a lead, Keith urged his teammates, a chance to pace his pitching. And forget strikeouts, Keith warned the hurler, especially when facing the weak hitters. Let them hit; you have a team behind you.

But any lineup made errors, and a miscue by Joe Pettus let in the first Bedford run. Tom seemed to take that as a challenge to his strikeout ability; anyhow he pitched himself out of that hole.

Rene had no such lapse in support; he breezed along until the third frame despite three singles. The Giants threatened then, filling the bases with only one away. But Jac's hard smash was grabbed by shortstop McMillan and turned into an out at home.

And Tom made the third out himself, fishing for a wide curve. His foot in the bucket like that, Keith thought unhappily—he couldn't have reached that pitch with a six-foot pole.

Then came another run for the Dodgers; Mart Kuhlman homered to the opposite field. That was the trouble about such fast pitching, Keith brooded. If the ball was just met squarely, over the fence it flew. Now the score stood 2–0.

At last, though, that goose egg was cracked. Keith doubled to left center, took third on a passed ball, then scored on the Little League version of a squeeze play—the batter bunting but the runner holding third until the throw to first, then coming home. It was close there, too; Keith's first thought was that he was out. But his desperate slide beat the tag, ruled the umpire, and Atlas was on the scoreboard at last.

But they were unable to pull into a tie, or even to hold the Dodgers scoreless from then on. For Tom weakened again in the sixth. Two hits, a walk, two passed balls, and two Dodger runners crossed the plate.

"All my fault," groaned Dick in the dugout.

That was true, of course; Keith could not deny it. But he knew from sad experience how difficult it was to hold or smother curves breaking wide and into the dirt.

Trailing four to one in the last frame, the Giants narrowed the gap on a homer by Roy Murray. Then Abe singled and Jac doubled to right center. It was 4–2, with a runner on second.

But there were two away and Tom Barton was due at the plate. Mr. Tracy stepped out of the dugout as the pitcher started for the batter's box.

"We'll let Joe hit for you, Tom," said the manager.

Tom started to protest, then managed to check himself. He dropped his bat and came back to the dugout and pulled on his warm-up jacket. Tight-lipped and sullen-eyed, he watched as Joe Weiman batted in his place.

Keith frowned. He sympathized with Tom, but also believed that Mr. Tracy had made the right move. Tom was no hitter and that was all there was to it. He could drag, sure; he was an expert at it. But the opposing defenses knew how to play him now, with the first sacker in tight and wide of the bag and the second baseman swung over to take the throw at first. And Joe was a good-hitting ten-year-old. He swung into the third pitch and hit a sharp line drive. Dewey Held caught it back-handed for the third out, but no fault could be found with Joe. When you hit it on the nose but right to somebody, there's nothing to do about it except wait for the next chance at bat.

The Giants in the cellar, no wins, two losses! Keith bit his lips as he joined his parents. And these were the two games he had been sure of winning!

"What your team needs is a little luck," his mother said comfortingly. "You haven't gotten any sort of break."

They hadn't, Keith agreed miserably. Two straight defeats—it just didn't make sense. Atlas boasted the best pitcher in the league, no doubt of it. Giant fielding was up to par. Three hitters had .333 averages. They were just jinxed, he decided. And Thursday, just day after tomorrow, they must face Calumet with Tom's allotted six innings a week used up.

Golly, who would pitch? Pat would start probably; the young "Four-eyes," as his teammates called him, had made fairly good showings in practice. But surely Mr. Tracy wasn't counting on Pat for a full game!

Keith did not follow his parents into the house, not immediately. He sat glumly on the front doorstep, still in his sweaty uniform, and struggled to recall every play of this shocking game. How had the Dodgers gotten four runs off Tom Barton? The pitcher had posted eleven strikeouts; he was well ahead of Merle Conroy's record for the season. He had given up two hits; the Giants had collected five off Rene. They were winning everywhere but on the scoreboard Keith decided in disgust.

He rose to go inside, but stopped as a car drove up in front of the Brush residence next door. He didn't recognize Sonny Barton until the singer stepped out of the car, waved to Keith, and walked briskly to the Brush front door. It was a rented car, Keith realized. And Sonny was wearing plain slacks and sports shirt. Except for his long hair, thought Keith with a smile, the rock-and-roller looked almost human. Then he thought about Tom, alone another night. Keith went straight to the telephone. Maybe Tom could come to his house, or he could go over there. Tom refused both suggestions. He was tired, he said. He meant to eat and go straight to bed.

Keith sighed. Tired? Of course, Tom was tired, but

Keith knew that wasn't the whole story. The olive-skinned boy took defeat hard, and now he had lost twice in the league he had expected to stand on its ear!

Pat Maguire *did* start. Furthermore, he held the Cats to two runs in three innings, no bad showing for a ten-year-old. Stout defense helped him, of course. This unusual Giant infield pattern held tight. Tom played deep and wide of third, Jac closer to second than most shortstops played— actually, decided Keith, they were using two shortstops. The setup appeared to leave the third base line wide open, but it wasn't. Tom could go to his right as easily as to his left, and, after backhanded catches, could throw well enough to get both runners. Keith had wondered why Mr. Tracy put his best infielder at third; it was clear now. Most third sackers played every ball they could reach, and that meant Tom ranging far into usual shortstop territory.

Dick Merrill could handle this young pitcher; the fact was, Keith could boast honestly, that this defensive lineup was airtight.

And hit—why hadn't they hit like this for Tom Barton? They treated Calumet's Louis Chastain like a cousin. Keith clouted his first home run in Little League; Roy Murray added another one.

After three innings the score stood Atlas 6, Calumet 2. Keith studied the scoreboard and shook his head. The Giants had dropped the two he had expected to win; now they led in a game he had been sure they would lose.

But it wasn't over, not by any means. Keith and Roy had warmed up both before the game and between turns at bat. Three innings would be all for Pat; Mr. Tracy had said so before the game. Keith held his breath as the manager hesitated an instant, then decided on Roy.

Roy threw just like a center fielder, overhanded, hard, accurately. He faced the weak end of the Cat batting order. He would get by the fourth with any kind of luck and if given the same sort of backing that Pat had had.

Frank Holmes belted out a single with one away. Billy Cox slashed one down the line; Tom came up with it somehow and threw off-balance to second. He could not have gotten the runner at first, but Joe speared the shaky peg barehanded and Frank was out at second.

Two away. Luke lifted a long fly to left; Dave pulled it in right against the fence.

Keith intercepted the grinning Roy on the way to the dugout. "Who said you couldn't pitch?"

"Shucks, everybody," the outfielder shrugged. "I just threw 'em over. Tom saved my hide."

His teammates felt the same way. More was made over Tom's fielding than his pitching, mused Keith. The swarthy boy drew a round of applause as he left the field. Color—Tom had it, thought Keith with some envy. He did everything gracefully except bat.

Billy Cox was pitching for Calumet now. They had knocked Chastain out of the box—the gloating comment passed around the Giant dugout. If they could handle this rookie the same way——

They couldn't. Billy was a carbon copy of Pat Maguire. The Giants connected with his sidearmed slants but hit right to waiting gloves. Keith flied out to deep center; for a while he thought he had hit his second homer. But the ball sailed high. Too much sky, Dave told him.

Keith nodded in rueful agreement.

Mr. Tracy's order surprised him. Abe Duran waited with mitt and ball. Keith gasped. Surely he wouldn't be sent to the mound. Roy had posted a scoreless inning. Why change pitchers?

"Their heavy end is up," the manager said tersely. "They would murder batting practice pitching."

Keith sighed and started throwing. What would the Cat sluggers do to him even if he could get the ball over?

He found out in an inning which seemed to stretch out forever. The Calumet aces couldn't hit him solidly! He walked Louis and Ruel in succession. Then, heart in his throat, he pitched to Mike Levy, the thick-set third baseman. Mike sort of sliced the ball; it caromed crazily toward right. Joe snatched it up and fired to Tom at third. One out.

Mike's twin brother, Josef, singled over third and one run scored. Keith threw four straight balls to Don Peterson, and the bases were full. Why didn't Mr. Tracy take him out?

The manager didn't stir. Keith licked his dry lips and kept his eyes fixed on Dick's mitt. If he could just get the ball over!

Five pitches later Keith had recorded his first Little League strikeout. But he managed only one strike against Holmes; the fourth ball sent Frank to first and another run across.

Tom Barton called time and came to the mound. "Just aim for the mitt," he advised. "Don't worry about putting anything on it."

Keith did not say what he was thinking, that Tom

should practice what he preached. Just aim for the mitt! Golly, what else was he doing!

"Strike one!"

"Strike two!"

Billy Cox had taken these two pitches. He swung at the third, chin-high and a little outside, and missed.

"Smart pitch," approved Tom.

Keith snorted as he hurried to the dugout. Smart pitch, the dickens! He had aimed right down the middle. He declined the windbreaker offered by José Aguirre. He was warm enough, certainly; in fact, sweat was streaming down his cheeks and neck—two kinds of perspiration, from heat and also from concern.

There were only three outs to go, but could he make it? The top of Calumet's batting order came up in the sixth.

"Get some more runs," he croaked to his teammates. "Get a batch of 'em."

The Giants did add one to their already impressive total. Keith trudged back to the mound with a four-run lead. He sighed as he faced Luke Doyle. Luke batted out of a crouch, making him hard to pitch to. And he was apt to hit any kind of pitch, too, even a freakish sidearmed offering which curved without the thrower's intent. Keith surely didn't want to walk the leadoff hitter. He stared at Dick's mitt, aimed carefully.

Luke took. They would all do that, of course. A wild pitcher—let him hang himself. Try to rattle him from the dugout. Pitcher's blowed—higher than a toad!

A ball, a second strike. Keith dared to try his palm pitch. It wobbled to the plate; Luke swung and topped the ball. It was shallow, a well-placed if unintentional bunt. Up swooped Tom. He grabbed the roller barehanded and pegged without rising up. Luke was out by a step.

Louis Chastain took first on a walk, Ruel Snead doubled to right field, the runner holding at third. The Giant infield kept deep, playing for the out, willing to let a run score. Mike Levy slashed a grounder past Keith. It would have been a safe hit except for the overshifted Atlas infield. Jac blocked the ball, picked it up and took two steps to second base.

Two gone, but there went Josef trotting to first after a fourth ball. Runners on first and third—Mr. Tracy signaled to play for Josef if he tried to take second. Keith threw high and outside, a perfect pitchout. There Josef went. And there streaked Dick Merrill's peg. It hit the dirt but Jac speared it well ahead of Josef. The Winston third-sacker turned and headed back to first. Ruel raced home unchallenged as the Giants concentrated on the rundown. Josef wasn't easy to trap, but finally Jac tagged him out. Keith had hurried to cover first; he took a deep breath and started for the dugout. His teammates swarmed around him, led by Tom. Gosh, protested the embarrassed pitcher, he hadn't done anything to be proud of.

But he had, said Mr. Tracy. He had pulled them through. Keith grinned ruefully. It seemed to him the Giants had won in spite of his pitching, not because of it. One win, two losses! They could hope now. Probably Tom would win every start from here on, especially if Atlas kept producing runs. And maybe he, Pat, and Roy could stagger other victories.

They would do better now, Mr. Tracy said confidently.

The manager stood talking to Keith's father and mother. The victory was a shot in the arm, he said.

That was sure true, agreed Keith. He no longer felt that the Giants were jinxed.

"Young Barton is something at third," Mr. Gregg said. "He may be even more valuable in the infield than as a pitcher."

"I'll make better use of his pitching from here on," Mr. Tracy said. "He can chunk, don't doubt that. His trouble is that he throws too much stuff for his size. He isn't too strong a boy, just about ninety pounds. He can't bear down for six full innings."

"Few boys can for a whole game," nodded Mr. Gregg. "I wish he could learn to pace himself."

"I thought I could teach him that," said the manager, "but I have failed so far." He showed a rueful smile. "I haven't been able to teach him anything so far. I'll use him from now on as did his Nashville coach—starting every game but going only three innings."

"Wouldn't you rather bring your strong pitcher in for the last three innings?"

"Sure. But Tom warms up slowly. He can't relieve at all." The coach's eyes twinkled. "I have his brother's word for that. Tom will help us more from now on, but not as much as we had expected. He isn't as good as he appears."

"I suppose that would be expecting too much," conceded Mr. Gregg.

"Entirely," said Mr. Tracy. "No boy is a team all by himself, no matter how hard he tries to be."

CHAPTER 11

O

The Giant Juggling Act

The second go-round started with the Giants against Winston and Bedford facing the Cats. The Crimson had upset the Dodgers to deadlock first place with two-one records. But Atlas and Calumet lagged only one game behind. The league picture could change entirely in this second full week.

The schedule allowed the Giants a practice session. Mr. Tracy devoted most of the two-hour period to batting practice and coaching his secondary pitching trio—Pat, Roy, and Keith. The former came in for little criticism; he threw as well as could be expected of a slight ten-year-old. But Keith did a hundred things wrong, especially coming off the mound. When he learned balance, said Mr. Tracy, he would have better control. And he must learn to gauge that unintentional wrinkle. Dick could help by holding an inside target; the catcher agreed.

Keith's delivery did bother hitters, even his own teammates.

"The danged curve comes in by way of third base," Roy said disgustedly. "You think it's going to hit you and then——"

Further words failed him. Keith grinned. If he worried Roy, then he could also puzzle others like Ruel Snead, Marty Kuhlman and even Doyle Chandler. By way of third base—Keith had not thought of that. But he did step off the rubber to his right, giving an angle to his throws, and making right-handed hitters pull and thus hit ground balls to either Tom or Jac, both sure fielders.

His angled pitches baffled Tom completely; a foot-in-the-bucket hitter had little chance of squarely meeting a sweeping break. Let him hit against Pat or Roy, asked Tom. Mr. Tracy shook his head.

"The sooner you learn to dig in, the quicker you can help us get runs. Sure Keith makes you look like a monkey. But you aren't out here to be babied."

Still another flash of those sullen dark eyes. Keith's lips twitched. How did Tom Barton feel now about the West Austin League? Didn't he rue the day his brother had decided to establish legal residence in this area? Tom couldn't be happy with his manager and teammates; he would smile more and swap friendly talk with the other boys if he was.

The usual taxi waited; Tom was in and gone just seconds after Mr. Tracy dismissed them. Keith and Dick walked slowly toward their respective homes.

"That Barton," grunted Dick. "What scares pitchers at the plate?"

"Pitchers hit just as well as anybody," Keith declared. "Look at Ruel, Dan, and Rene."

Dick conceded the point. "But Barton sure can't."

"No, but he can pitch and play infield. If you could hold him better——"

"There's no holding him when he tires out," answered Dick with a shrug. "He is too tough to catch any time, but along in the fifth or sixth inning—he sort of gets mad when he starts losing his stuff and tries to chunk even harder."

"Mr. Tracy knows that," Keith said tersely. "But you have to admit Tom is the league's best pitcher for four or five innings."

"Sure," Dick agreed quickly. His blue eyes gleamed. "And you know who is our best catcher now, outside of you."

"You are hustling," Keith agreed. "That's all you ever had to do."

They separated at Pecos Street; Keith trudged on alone. Practices, he reflected, were more tiring than games. Well, maybe not for catchers; he remembered his ordeals of the previous year. But that was still the position to play—more action and excitement, more fun than being a sidearmed pitcher, even if his new way of throwing did bother hitters.

He found his parents in the den, both absorbed by television. Sonny Barton was on again, minus the showy costume.

"Your supper is all ready."

So it was; for several minutes Keith was too occupied to think about the television fare. But it finally occurred to him to tease his father.

"I thought you didn't care for Sonny's yowling."

"I appreciate folk music when it's good," Mr. Gregg said

without turning his head, "and, for some reason, Sonny Barton omits rock-and-roll from his television repertory."

Keith's eyes twinkled. Probably, he mused, he was the only twelve-year-old boy in West Austin who understood his father's every word. And that was only because he was so accustomed to a lawyer's way of saying things.

"The reason lives next door," his mother put in. "However, I understand Sonny has had a date with Luke's sister also. Has Luke mentioned that, son?"

"Not to me," Keith said. "And I won't say anything about it to him," he added after some thought. "Luke has a temper. He might want to fight."

A chuckle came from Mr. Gregg. "I count my blessings every so often," he said gently. "One of them is that I don't have a teen-aged daughter to worry about."

The Crimson tried to beat the Giants with Seth Mitchell, their second pitcher, and save Rene for the second game that week. That gave Mr. Tracy a talking point and he made the most of it.

"We have been the team to beat in this league ever since it was started," he said in the dugout. "Now we are treated like cousins. Throw the second best pitcher against Atlas, save the ace for Calumet. Are we going to have that kind of season?"

"No, sir," promised fifteen earnest voices.

Seth was an oversized, slow-moving, friendly blond boy. He boasted fair speed and a curve, but only Tom Barton failed to hit him in the first three innings.

Tom's pitching, however, made up for his failure at the plate. The several days of rest had helped him, Keith decided. This was like the early innings of the opening game; most Crimson hitters came up and went back to their dugout without even touching the ball. Tom racked up seven strikeouts, not a single runner reaching first.

Meanwhile the Giants had four scores on eight base hits!

Pat had been warming up since the second inning; Keith and Roy had thrown, too. Pat took over the mound at the start of the fourth.

Tom was displeased, and showed it. But his feelings did not interfere with his fielding. He darted across the infield to grab a slow-rolling hit and account for the first out. Pat let the Reds hit; he could not help it. Doyle homered but Wingo flied out to end the rally.

Dan took the mound. Keith, waiting in the circle, looked to Mr. Tracy. Winston had been forced to bring in its ace; the Giants had done that much, anyhow. Coach Chase Alloway of the Reds was sure going for broke. Now he must go three-three in the second game of the week, which might well mean two defeats and elimination from the first half scramble.

On the other hand, if the Reds came back to win this game—Atlas could use Tom Barton for only three innings against the league-leading Dodgers! We have to hold this lead, Keith grunted. Let this one get away and we're in the slough ourselves.

Dan set the Giants down in order. Pat Maguire trudged back to the box, resumed his careful pitching.

He kept cool, even against a lineup hitting him hard and able to pull. And the same factor which helped Keith benefited Pat. Most of Winston's plate power was right-handed. The batters who tagged the slow offerings hit toward left, toward Tom and Jac in the infield, to Dave in left, or Roy playing well over in left center. And Pat walked no one. The bespectacled boy had unusual control.

Stout fielding rescued him, too, but only after two runs in that awful fifth inning. Four-three! We need runs, croaked Keith, first in the dugout.

Mr. Tracy sent both him and Roy to the bullpen. Their warm-up was short; Dan got the Giants out in one-two-three order. Keith looked hopefully to his tall manager. Winston's last two hitters were due up, neither strong with the stick. Both would probably be taking.

Mr. Tracy granted Keith's unspoken plea. The substitution sent Abe to left, Dave to center, and Roy to the mound. Three quick pitches proved the strategy sound. David Baker took two strikes, then lifted a short fly to left center. Keith held his breath as he watched the sinking ball. Abe must really move to get it. Joe Pettus called the straining Jacques back; all eyes watched Duran's desperate try. He grabbed the ball and tumbled on his face. But he held on and there was one out. Still another time Keith wagged his head and whispered appreciation of Abe's value to the team.

Two to go, Keith whooped to his teammates. Let's get 'em out and go home!

But Ron Bellamy proved a better hitter than they expected. He connected squarely and sent a line drive over third.

The top of the Crimson batting order was up now with the tying run at first. Mr. Tracy stepped out of the dugout and gestured Keith to the mound and Roy to first.

Keith licked his lips. Now he must prove his control

under pressure and also the effectiveness of his sidearmed slants. Last week he had staggered through because of a big lead. Now he had no margin of error at all. Let this base runner move on around and the score was tied.

Five warm-up throws, then Keith nodded that he was ready. Steve Kalumas crowded the plate, crouching. He was sure to take, sighed Keith. He gestured for even more of an inside target. If he could get the first one over, force Steve to hit——

Steve fell away from the pitch, but the umpire gestured a strike. Another one came in almost in the same spot. The Crimson leadoff man stepped out of the box, upset by these two calls. But both pitches got the inside corner even if they had started straight at the batter. Steve rubbed his hands in the dirt and stepped back in. Now Keith could bait the batter. He decided on his palm ball. Let it drift outside; Steve might cut anyhow.

He did, and topped the ball. Keith hurried to pick it up. Dick was out from behind the plate.

"First base," yelled the catcher.

Keith turned and threw carefully to Roy. Two gone.

"You might have gotten him at second," said Dick, "but I wanted to be sure of one."

Keith nodded. That was the play, all right.

Now came Eddie Wilson. Keith's first two efforts slanted wide in spite of his best efforts. He licked his lips and managed to put a strike across. But two more balls sent Eddie to first and brought Dan up.

Keith called for time and squeezed the resin bag. The go-ahead runs were on base, and Winston's two best batters ready. Keith respected Dan but meant to avoid pitching to

Doyle if he possibly could. Dan might be hitting away; if so, anything fat might well end up against the fence or even over it.

He threw hard and the extra effort brought a wider slant. Dan was clear out of the box when the ball thudded into Dick's mitt. The umpire did not hesitate; up went his right hand.

The same spot, whispered Keith. He gestured for Tom to move closer to the base and Duran to shift toward the left-field foul line. He toed the rubber and took careful aim——

Crack! Dan connected for sure. He laced a curving line drive several feet over Tom's head. But Abe Duran was squarely in position to take the hit. All he had to do was gauge its break and squeeze the spinning ball in his glove.

Here he came, running to the dugout. Keith licked his dry lips and grinned weakly at Eddie, hurrying over with congratulations.

"Just luck," the pitcher said modestly. "I thought you had us."

And he had thought so until he saw Abe's immediate reaction to the hit. Apparently the Giant utility handy-andy player had never doubted for an instant that he could make the catch.

The Giants' season record stood at two-two now, tied with the Crimson. If Calumet could just upset Bedford— the Giants worried as much about that game as their own practice. Mr. Tracy let them go after hitting and throwing drill. The practice was at the playground, almost a mile from Knebel Field. It was not yet six o'clock; they could watch the final inning or two if they could find rides to the park. Mr. Tracy could take most of them in his station wagon; Tom invited the others to crowd into the waiting taxi.

"Won't this cost extra?" worried Keith.

Tom shrugged. He wasn't sure; he never paid the fare anyhow. Sonny had an arrangement with the taxi company. But what if it did?

The fifth inning was just starting. One look at the scoreboard set off a chorus of whoops. Calumet led 3–1. Ruel Snead was besting Rene Ramirez! Golly, gloated Keith, everything was going their way, even Mac Collins' pitching choices. Now Rene could not work against Atlas in the next game!

The Giants sat together but Mr. Tracy gave strict instructions about cheering for either team. But they could hope, and whisper together, and there was no erasing their grins as the scoreboard totals went unchanged. Larry Cripps fanned for the last out.

"Now," announced Mr. Thomas, "we have a unique situation in the West Austin League, all four teams tied for first place."

But not for long, chortled Keith, not unless he and Pat failed in their relief duties. For there was no doubting what Tom Barton would do in the first three innings of their next game.

The taxi waited, its meter running all this time, to Keith's dismay.

"I forgot about it," Tom confessed. He shrugged his shoulders. "Since it's here, you might as well ride home."

Keith accepted. Why was it a thrill to share the back seat

of a taxi? The Gregg car was a newer and more comfortable model, but it sort of made him feel important, stepping out of the cab and nodding to the driver. He couldn't help envying Tom for an instant. How many other twelve-year-olds kept taxis waiting while they watched the final innings of a Little League game?

CHAPTER 12

O

Two Hollow Victories

Mr. Tracy called all fifteen Giants into the dugout.

"You believe you can hit Billy Harper and you can," he said sternly. "But you can't cut from your heels and do anything with his 'junk.' He is like Pat and Keith—the harder you swing against him, the more you pop up and top the ball. He is a better pitcher than he looks; be sure of that. Now start us off, Jac."

The shortstop worked Harper to a 2–1 count, then forgot his manager's warning. Jac swung at the next offering as if determined to lose the ball in the trees. He got wood on it, all right, but lofted a rainmaker which Bart French caught in deep center field.

Tom Barton was next. "Get on somehow," Keith urged. But he had little hope of that; the swarthy boy had yet to record a solid base hit. Except for two successful drags, he had been horse-collared in four full games. But batting-cage sessions, humiliation in practice as he pulled away from

Keith's slants, perhaps confidence against a "second" pitcher—who knew what made a hitter click? Tom met the first pitch squarely for a single into center field.

Joe Pettus now. Keith watched Tom anxiously, praying that his teammate would not go down on his own again. Mr. Tracy would blow a fuse if that happened; he had warned Tom once.

Joe sent a humpbacked safety into left center. Instructed to pick one out, Keith went to the plate. He connected solidly but first-sacker Cripps knocked the ball down and then managed to beat Keith to the bag.

Both runners moved up, but two were gone. Keith relieved Tim Haley of coaching duties and called encouragement to Dave.

The outfielder came through. His sharp roller through the mound and past second scored two tallies. Roy hit right back to Harper for an easy third out.

But who couldn't be happy over two runs in the lead-off inning? Keith took a lob from shortstop LeClerc and handed the ball to Tom.

"Good hitting," he praised the pitcher.

"Sonny should have seen it," Tom said with a grin. "He won't believe me when I tell him."

"I'll swear to it. Now fog it in there. This is *the* ball game for us."

"We'll win it," Tom said confidently.

Atlas would hold their lead until the late innings; Keith was sure of that. For Tom struck out the first two batters and Dick caught a high foul almost against the wire for the third out.

The Giants failed to score in the second as Jac popped

up with two away and Dick on third base. The towhead had doubled, then moved up on a passed ball.

Keith passed Dick coming to the dugout for his pads. "I'm even with you now," grinned the catcher. "I'm up to .333."

That was good hitting for a receiver, agreed Keith. He was a good mitt man, too. Abe's catching future seemed settled; he would be kept ready in case of an emergency. Otherwise he would alternate between third base and left field. Getting Tom and Abe in the auction, Dick's improvement, his own pitching despite an awkward new throwing style—all those things have made us into a title threat again, mused Keith.

Tom walked Marty Kuhlman. Keith started toward the mound but stopped. It was nothing to worry about; Tom had given fewer free passes than any other hurler.

A curve got away from Dick, and Marty took second standing up. Larry Cripps had swung and missed; Dick should have had no trouble with the throw. Now Keith did call soothingly to the mound. It worried any pitcher when his receiver could not hold his Sunday pitches.

"You got him on your hip," Keith sung out.

Larry swung left-handed and rated among the league's best hitters. He showed why on the next offering. He waited out Tom's palm ball and slashed a wicked hopper toward Keith.

He scooped it out of the dirt in time to play the runner streaking for third, if he hurried and threw right on the money.

Abe took the knee-high peg and braced for Marty's slide.

There was no way the runner could avoid the tag. Marty scrambled up and crossed the infield to the Dodger dugout.

"Good boy, Abe," yelped Keith, as he moved back to his position. "We're with you, Tom boy. Just keep——"

Keith gasped with sudden realization of how he had thrown to third. Overhanded, that was how! He tested his arm and there was neither pain nor stiffness. How had it happened?

"What's the matter?" asked Tom, coming over from the box.

Mr. Tracy came out of the dugout, too. Was he hurt? Keith shook his head.

"See how I threw?" he asked a bit hoarsely. "Overhanded. And it didn't hurt at all. See?" He swung his arm and his grin stretched from ear to ear. "The doctor was wrong," he said. "It not only can get well, it is well."

"Don't take any chances," cautioned the manager. He tapped Tom's shoulder. "You, either. Weak hitters coming up. Try again to pace yourself."

"Yes, sir," agreed Tom.

But he struck out Billy and Dewey with the same stuff—fast balls, sharp curves. Dick's passed balls let Larry advance to third but he died there.

The relief brigade took to the bullpen with Dick and Abe catching. Keith could not resist an overhanded effort. The motion was no strain at all. Now, he gloated, he could really pitch. He was throwing "off his ear" as well as ever. And, mixing overhanded fast balls with his slants by way of third——

The Giant reliefers had their work cut out for them, for Harper held them scoreless. Two-nothing going into the fourth. Abe yielded third base to Tom and sat out until Keith should take the mound. That special substitution rule saved them, thought Keith. What if this was like professional ball and Abe could not return to the lineup?

He wanted to pitch. He found himself almost hoping that Pat would falter.

But the ten-year-old had different ideas. Pat's junk handcuffed the Dodgers through the fourth and fifth frames. Meanwhile Atlas added another run; it was 3–0 as Bedford came to bat in the sixth.

Pat walked Rene Ramirez. Marty singled sharply, Rene holding at second.

Mr. Tracy waited no longer. Keith went to the mound, Roy to first, Abe to the outfield. How many times did this happen in Little League, mused Keith as he took his warm-up throws? A pitcher relieved before he had allowed a run!

He tried his overhanded fast ball twice. Dick came to the mound.

"You got your arm back!" he exclaimed.

Keith grinned. He sure did. They had better revise their signals then, said the catcher. One for an overhanded fast ball, two for sidearmed, three for a curve, closed fist for the palm ball. Keith nodded. Four pitches—he should be able to keep the hitters guessing.

Larry hit to Keith who played for first. Three runs ahead, get the big out. Billy took a strike, an overhanded pitch. Then the Dodger hurler poked a grounder to third. Tom, from regular depth, ignored the runner streaking home and pegged to Roy. Two gone. Dewey Held scored the second run with a Texas leaguer into right center. But Jim Burns struck out and the game was over.

Mr. Thomas's announcement set off a second demonstration by the blue-capped boys.

"The Giants now hold first place with three games won and two lost."

They would share the top rung with the next day's victor, of course, but what a change since opening week, since losing their first two games despite Tom's great pitching!

His arm—his mother's eyes moistened. "If it doesn't hurt, I'm sure it's all right to throw that way. But let's check with Dr. Martin to be sure."

The physician promised to stop by the Gregg house while making other calls. He probed Keith's arm from wrist to shoulder, then shook his near-bald head.

"To put it in simple language," he explained, "the dead nerves have come back to life. It isn't a miracle, especially not for a twelve-year-old boy who would not accept a practical diagnosis—that he would never regain full use of his arm."

"I knew I would," Keith said. "I *had* to."

"There is your explanation," Dr. Martin said with a smile.

"You don't think there is any risk——"

"The arm is as sound as ever," said Dr. Martin with a shrug.

Then he could go back to catching, except for relief stints on the mound! Or could he? He sighed. Did he even want to—this year? Dick was doing well enough. He was not holding Tom's Sunday stuff too well, but then who could? And who would play first base if Keith put on the pads again? Mr. Tracy might refuse to juggle a winning combination.

And that was exactly what the manager decided, for the time being, anyhow.

"We are clicking on all eight," said Mr. Tracy. "We will practice you some behind the plate and see how Dick takes to first. We have to play him somewhere. We need his hitting and hustle. However," he considered, "you would be a cinch to make the all-star team as a catcher. This way—I just don't know. You can't beat out Doyle at first. And pitching——"

He did not have to finish; Keith nodded. The league boasted several better hurlers. All he had done so far was hang on to leads behind Tom's pitching.

"We have to think about the team first," he said without hesitation.

"Sure," nodded the manager. "Probably the all-star business will take care of itself. The other coaches usually recognize leadership. And while Tom is our outstanding player, I think they know who holds this club together."

The Cats won a 3–2 thriller to claim a share of the lead. Their victory pleased Keith and his teammates, for Ruel Snead pitched all six innings. Coach Sneaker Kane must depend on Louis Chastain or Hal Sumner against the Giants, while Mr. Tracy could use his same pitching pattern.

"We are getting every break in the world," the tall manager told his players. "Let's make hay while we can. We have it easy after this week."

Every blue-capped boy knew what he meant. The other

coaches had counted Atlas out of the first half and had revised their pitching schedules accordingly. But not any more. The West Austin League, gloated Keith, was back to normal, with the Giants the team to beat.

They tore into Louis, hitting for four runs in the first two innings. Keith's home run scored Joe Pettus ahead of him—this must be what people meant, he thought as he circled the bases, by somebody's cup running over! That fitted things to a T. Everything was going his way.

Mr. Tracy put Pat in for the third frame, to Keith's great satisfaction. Now Tom Barton could go four innings against Winston instead of three. This one, then a win over the Crimson—pull that off and the Giants were going downhill.

Pat got by the third well enough. But in the next inning, Luke singled and Ruel homered over the left field wall.

Mr. Tracy did not hesitate. Let the opposing batters time their swings to Pat's slow stuff and the ten-year-old was no longer effective.

Keith was purposely deliberate with his warm-ups. He had met every relief test thus far, but this was sterner than the others. He had to protect a two-run lead for two and two-thirds innings. And he had to start against the Levy twins, both capable hitters.

Mike came up taking, for which Keith was grateful. He could put his overhanded effort right over and did. The advantage of a called strike was no small one; it let the pitcher try his breaking stuff. Mike swung at the sidearmed roundhouse and poked a grounder to Joe for the second out.

Josef doubled down the line, cutting at the first pitch.

But Keith worked confidently against lanky Don Peterson. The Cat first-sacker fell away from the pitch, as had Tom Barton until this week. Keep the ball outside, preferably high—Keith had such control with his natural straight-through delivery. Don popped up to Jac and the rally was squelched.

Another run for Atlas; now Keith had a 5–2 margin to work on. And good fielding support, besides his control against weaker hitters. He would give up few walks from here on, and his own wildness had kept him in hot water in previous games.

He was hit, sure. Frank Holmes and Luke rapped out singles. Mike Levy homered in the sixth, and Preston Adair sliced a double down the right field foul line.

But all this stick work produced only two runs and Joe's homer made the final score 6–4. Two more victories would cinch a tie for the first half even if one of the other teams won three straight.

Don't count your chickens too soon, his father warned him on the way home. You won't get as many runs from here on.

True, nodded Keith, all too true. If Tom could go the full route—the schedule would let him work against Winston, then a full game against either the Dodgers or the Cats, whichever showed up as the stronger threat. Keith sighed. A win over the Reds would just set the stage for a showdown game. And how they would need their pitching ace for all six innings of that!

The telephone was ringing as Keith and his parents entered the house.

"For you," Mrs. Gregg told her husband after hurrying to answer it.

Keith dropped into a chair and groped through the afternoon newspaper for the sports section. He paid no attention to his father's part of the telephone conversation until——

"Why, Sonny, that shocks me—Yes, I remember that you mentioned some cancellations but—I realize that—two weeks *would* cause a financial crisis with your overhead——"

Now Keith was all ears and concern.

"——Of course, Sonny—ten o'clock in the morning—But I still hope that something can be worked out—You are happy here and Tom is doing so well in Little League—Very well, Sonny, ten o'clock. Good-by."

Mrs. Gregg had overheard enough to be waiting anxiously, too.

"What is it, dear?"

"Curtains for the Giants, I'm afraid," he said tersely. "Sonny Barton has had two one-week engagements canceled. The summer slump has hit, as he feared it would."

Keith shuddered. "He isn't—leaving——?"

"He must," Mr. Gregg said tonelessly. "He has no promise of bookings in this area until September, when schools reopen, vacations and the outdoor season are over. He finishes up at the Plantation Club Saturday. He can open in Nashville next Monday night."

"But if he leaves, then Tom——"

"Is lost to the Giants," his father confirmed. He sighed. "You will have him for one more game."

"But not for the last week, and that's when——!"

"I know," Mr. Gregg nodded. He forced a smile. "Now you can understand why the other managers let Jim Tracy take him at a reasonable price."

Tears welled in Keith's eyes. "We can't win without him. We won't stand a chance. Even when he isn't pitching——"

"He is also the mainstay of your defense and is beginning to hit," Mr. Gregg shook his head. "It is too bad, for the boy's sake."

The doorbell rang. Mrs. Gregg rose to admit Dick Merrill.

"You may as well join the wake, Dick," she said. "Keith is about to cry and I am not far from it myself."

"Let's go outside," Keith said tonelessly. "I can tell him better out there."

Dick sat on the curb to hear the dismaying news.

"Golly," he whispered hoarsely. "We can't stand it. He is—I still don't like him much—but he is——"

"The difference between our winning and losing," Keith finished glumly.

"Things were going so good," grieved Dick. "Your arm getting well—I want you to start catching again. But I don't suppose—gosh, if we could have him just one more week——"

He stopped himself, fairly springing to his feet. "I've got it!" he whooped. "My dad can book Sonny at his club for next week! That would get us through the first half. And, even if we didn't win the second half, we would be in a one-game playoff for the championship. By then, the way you are pitching——"

"Will your father do it?"

"We can ask him," shrugged Dick. "In fact, we can do more than just *ask*. You come and help me."

Keith hesitated, then nodded. He was willing to ask Mr. Merrill. Dick's father was always pleasant and soft-spoken. But not convinced at once that the Club Caravan should engage Sonny Barton for a week. In fact, quite to the contrary.

"I have not lost my mind over Little League baseball," he said firmly. "Not quite, anyhow. The Club Caravan appeals to older people with conservative tastes. Bring in a rock-and-roll hit! Why, we would get none of our regular customers. We would be stormed by bobby soxers, instead, and we don't want *their* business."

"But just a week," Dick begged. "And it is the off season for the club. You said so this morning."

"But Barton's fee is the same," countered Mr. Merrill. "His act is really too high priced for us anytime." He paused and took a deep puff on his cigar.

"However," he mused, "there is the publicity angle. If he does not draw at all, that would get into the newspapers. It would be good advertising for us. And it *would* be expense that we could count off the income tax."

Keith had given up easily; now he raised his head in new hope. After firmly refusing the idea, Mr. Merrill was considering it.

"We will think about it," he promised after another minute's consideration. "Let me talk it over with the club manager and our publicity man. It does not have to be done tonight, I hope?"

"No, sir," Keith conceded. He gulped. "But the sooner we know, the better we will all feel. It takes something out of us—trying to win and worrying about our best pitcher at the same time."

"I understand," Mr. Merrill said with a smile. "There is the team's morale. I shall keep that in mind. The Giants have a fine drive going. I want to see you take this first half, anyhow."

"We can win it, with Tom," Keith said.

"I will do what I can," promised Mr. Merrill.

The gleam in his eyes satisfied Keith. There was no doubting that Mr. Merrill wanted to solve this emergency facing the team.

CHAPTER 13

O

Exit the Bartons

And he did, as far as the Club Caravan was concerned. The booking was arranged next morning. Dick came pedaling over on his bicycle to give Keith the great news.

"Dad's publicity man thinks it is a great idea," Dick explained. "The more empty tables, he says, the more free advertising for the club, maybe even in the national magazines. The club is announcing the booking on radio and television already."

"Then we are set for the first half," Keith gloated.

Sure enough Keith, watching a sports special, saw and heard the first advertisement. Mr. Gregg did not, but he knew about the engagement by noon. In fact, he came home for lunch because of it. He asked a few quick questions and soon knew about the roles of Keith and Dick in the booking.

"I am sorry to menace your playhouse," he said sternly. "But the league directors must know about this."

154

"Why?" blinked Keith. "Is there some sort of rule——?"

"No," said Mr. Gregg a bit sharply. "I am sure there is no rule exactly covering this situation. Who would have thought it would ever come up? But I feel that this special booking violated the spirit of Little League, and I intend to vote so."

"Dad!" protested Keith.

The lawyer gestured with both hands. "That is my conviction. I was willing to concede that a singer has as much right to relocate his headquarters as anybody else. That was discussed by the directors and I defended Sonny's right to change his home address. I pointed out that we cannot challenge a professional man, such as a lawyer or an author, who decided that he wanted to live in West Austin." He sighed. "But this—offering employment to keep a player eligible for another week—that is putting too much emphasis on Little League, especially on winning."

"But, Dad," Keith said almost tearfully, "if we don't have Tom——"

"Your father is right, son," Mrs. Gregg said softly but firmly. "He is the league's players' agent. His responsibility is to the league."

"To *all* Little Leagues," Mr. Gregg added.

"What will you do?" asked Keith hopelessly.

"As players' agent I shall ask the directors to decide whether or not this booking violates the principles of Little League."

"But, gosh, Dad, we practice tomorrow and play Winston Friday——"

"I consider him eligible for *that* game," the attorney

said. "Sonny's bookings through this week should not concern the board. But this Club Caravan arrangement——"

He shook his head. "In my opinion," he declared, "we should not allow Tom to play an extra week by special arrangement with Mr. Merrill."

Keith lowered his head. Further argument was useless and he knew it. Besides, he had to concede that his father was probably right. Mr. Gregg usually was. And, if it had not been for him and Dick, Mr. Merrill would have not even known that Sonny Barton had no more bookings in the Austin area.

"Now not a word about this," the lawyer told his son sharply, "until the league has acted. Do you promise?"

Keith took a deep breath. "Yes, sir," he said reluctantly.

Tom could pitch four innings against Winston. That was enough in itself to make the Giants confident of their fifth straight victory.

What if Dan Poggin was starting for the Reds and could go the full distance? The Giants had scored off Dan and would again. Keith, warming up briefly before the game, felt that he was throwing even better than last year. He could control his palm ball and, when he tried a curve, the ball broke some. He felt that he could get out the Reds if needed for relief. He told Mr. Tracy so.

"Fine," said the manager. "But don't give up that side-arm all at once. That step toward third and your dinky curve—it worries the weaker hitters."

Keith rejoined his teammates in the dugout. All of the Giants were in high spirits. A win today could cinch at least a first half tie with two contests left. For if the Giants beat the Reds and then the Cats won over Bedford the next day, the other three teams would have 3–4 records. Atlas would have a 5–2 standing.

Of course, if this was Tom Barton's last game—Keith bit his lips. Why even guess about it? It would be. The other directors would agree with Mr. Gregg.

He shot a sidewise glance at Mr. Tracy. Surely the manager knew that the board meant to vote on Tom's status. But Keith must not say anything or even hint that he knew about such a prospect. He had promised his father so.

The Atlas manager warned his players to expect strong opposition.

"You will have to earn this one," he said sternly. "The Reds have their backs to the wall. They won't give up. They have their best pitcher eligible for the full six innings. Be on your toes and grab every break you can reach."

Winston proved in the first inning that the Reds were out to win. With one away, Eddie Wilson singled to right field. He took second and then third on successive passed balls.

Wide pitches both, breaking into the dirt and getting away from Dick.

Keith asked for time and went to the mound. Tom stood there scowling.

"Just get it over," Keith said soothingly. "Nobody hurt."

The pitcher shook his head. "Dick can't hold my curve," he complained. "If we could have kept the runner on first——"

"Try your fast one."

"I have to," muttered Tom. "Even if it is Chandler."

The infield was in shallow, of course, hoping for a play at

the plate. The outfield was stationed deep out of respect for Chandler's stick ability. He might take this 2–0 pitch, thought Keith. Tom was known around the league for tiring. Mr. Alloway of the Reds might decide to make the Atlas hurler throw as many pitches as possible. With——

Chandler's bunt came as a surprise. The batter did not give away his intention, as did most Little League hitters. He simply flicked a trailer toward third.

Both Abe and Tom scrambled for the ball.

"Tom!" yelled Dick Merrill, whipping off his mask and guarding home plate.

The third baseman sprang back to let the pitcher have the chance.

"First base!" shouted Dick.

It was the wrong call. At least, Tom did it wrong. He should have driven the runner back to third before making his throw. Doyle Chandler might have beaten such a delayed peg, but at least——

For, on the throw, Eddie Wilson tore for home. Keith was up for the bunt and Joe covered first. Joe threw to Dick but Eddie slid in under the mitt and was safe.

Two away. Keith called that to his slightly ruffled teammates. Doyle Chandler swung at a curve and missed. The ball got away from Dick again. No harm was done with no runner to advance, but Tom showed disgust anyhow. He used only fast balls to get out the Winston cleanup hitter. Doyle hit a 2–1 pitch into deep right center which Davis Gordon caught almost against the fence.

"Let's get that one back," yelled Jac, running in to grab a bat.

"Get on," Joe promised. "We will knock you in."

But pitcher Dan Poggin had different ideas. He retired the Giants one-two-three. Tom fanned for the second out, swinging from his heels. Keith scowled. Was something wrong with their star this game? It was not like Tom to overswing, try to kill the ball.

One-nothing, Winston's favor. Tom used only his fast ball through the second frame. He struck out one batter. Duke Canfield reached first on what was scored a single, though it was no clean hit. Jac failed to charge a slow trickler with his usual speed. Keith sighed in relief as Seth Mitchell fouled out to Abe to retire the side. Keith could not help but worry. His teammates did not seem to have their usual spirit.

And Poggin was "right" on the mound; that was for sure. No Atlas batter reached first base in the second inning, either.

Nor the third. Still 1–0 as Tom walked slowly to the mound for the first half of the fourth, his final inning of the week.

Doyle Chandler was leading off for Winston. He hit a 2–0 pitch through the box for a single. Tobe Wingo advanced the runner with a sacrifice. Dan now, a strong hitter in addition to his mound ability. The count reached 2–2.

Curve him, whispered Keith.

Apparently Dick called for a breaking pitch. But Tom shook off the signal. Keith kicked at the dirt. A curve might get away from Dick, true, but, even so, the runner would only take third——

——Instead of scoring! For Dan met the fast pitch squarely and poked a humpbacked liner just over Keith's mitt. Doyle scored from the second and the Reds led 2–0.

That was all the damage as Duke struck out and Davis popped up to Joe.

But 2–0, with Tom's total of six innings a week used up! Keith called hoarsely to Joe Pettus, starting the Atlas half of the fourth. If the Giants lost this one and faced the final two games without Tom—it could be calamity!

"Start something, Joe."

Pat Maguire was warming up. He would take Weiman's place in the batting order, guessed Keith. And the slight Pat was near helpless at the plate. Atlas hitting strength suffered with him in the lineup.

"Get on, Joe," Keith yelled a bit frantically. This *had* to be the inning.

But it was not. Pettus, Dave, and Keith went out in order. The best Keith could manage was a hard grounder directly at the second baseman.

Pat managed to hold the Reds in the fifth, though Steve singled with two gone.

Keith studied the scoreboard as he went to warm up for a possible pitching turn. There was no way he could change the figures. Two-nothing it was with the Giant "weak end" coming up. Even if Dave got on, there was Pat up next. Would Mr. Tracy try a pinch hitter if that happened? There was Roy Murray available, slowed slightly by a turned ankle, but able to hit.

Davis did reach first. He punched a roller through the hole at short and third. Try Roy, whispered Keith.

But Mr. Tracy made no move to stop Pat Maguire as the young pitcher marched to the plate. Keith stopped throwing to watch. Pat seldom swung at bad pitches. If only Dan would walk his opposing pitcher——

A called strike instead. Keith bit his lips. Dan was just getting the ball over against this weak hitter.

Pat swung around in the box and bunted. His trickler toward first spun crazily and then stopped dead. Pat was speedy afoot; he beat Dan's throw by a half-step.

Keith yelled in delight. Now if only Dick——

The very first pitch removed that "if." The Winston defense had moved in slightly, to double play depth, or to be prepared for a bunt.

And that was what Keith expected, Mr. Tracy's signal to move up the runners, to put the tying runs in scoring position.

But no such thing. Dick took a full cut instead. And he connected—no doubt of that. Keith followed the ball's flight breathlessly. It was deep and high and right to center fielder Mitchell. Seth would probably pull it in, but, back so deep, there might be an advance to third. And, on the throw——

No! Dick's fly kept soaring instead of sinking. It finally dropped, but beyond Seth's reach.

It fell over the chain link fence for a home run!

Yippee! Keith went back to throwing with a wide grin splitting his face. Good old Dick! Three-two now, Atlas ahead. What a home run!

He told Dick so as the Giants took the field.

The stocky catcher just grunted.

What was wrong with his friend, worried Keith? Dick should be floating on air instead of crouching with his mask only partially hiding his scowl. Then Keith realized the cause of the catcher's unusual attitude. Those early passed balls—Tom Barton had made it plain—had even said it—

that the catcher was responsible. The swarthy boy had shook off curve signals because he could not trust his receiver's ability, and had made it plain why he was doing so.

Then Keith had more than this to worry him.

Doyle Chandler walked on six pitches. Pat had pitched carefully, aiming low and outside. The slight boy was throwing well—no hurler took chances with Doyle—but still Chandler personified the tying run.

And young Pat must be just as careful not to groove one for Tobin Wingo. His curve was missed. It dipped low and into the dirt. Dick blocked it with a desperate lunge.

"Nice catching, boy," Keith yelled.

"I was ready to go down," muttered Doyle, coming back to stand at first.

Two successive balls.

"You got to get this one in there, Pat, boy," Keith called.

The pitcher touched the resin bag, faced the hitter. His roundhouse broke in and down——

The hit and run was on! Doyle streaked for second the instant the ball reached the plate.

Tobin swung and missed. And now Dick's peg. Keith watched, heart in his mouth. So far Merrill's throwing had been erratic, and never strong. But this shot was right into Jac's glove. The shortstop braced himself for Doyle's slide. LeClerc went sprawling but held on to the ball and the runner was out.

One away. Keith yelled that in a shrill voice.

Now two out as Wingo hit an easy hopper to Joe.

Only Dan Poggin left. It was not over yet, Keith reminded his teammates. Dan crouched well up in the box, ready to clout Pat's offering before it broke.

And hit he did, a streaking liner toward left field. It

would have been a clean hit against any team but Atlas. Tom Barton, though, made the catch look fairly easy. He leaped up, speared the ball glove-handed and the game was over.

Keith ran to hug Dick. "You won that for us," he said happily.

"Sure," Dick said with a proud grin. "Tom Barton isn't the whole show. He just thinks he is."

Tom, not two steps away, heard every word.

"If you could catch," he snapped at Dick, "we never would have been behind."

"Stop that stuff," Keith ordered. "Let us tell them they played a good game."

He led the Giant parade over to the Winston dugout.

Keith was too thrilled over this victory to worry more about the ill feeling between star pitcher and catcher. For the moment, that was. He led the team in the usual circle of the field and helped load the equipment into Mr. Tracy's car. Then he and Dick started homeward.

They were a block from the field when a taxicab braked to a stop by them and Tom Barton sprang out.

"You won the game for us with your homer," he told Dick grimly. "But I didn't like those cracks about me. I don't think you are *trying* to hold my curves."

"I can't help it because you are wild," Dick said with a shrug.

"You could *stop* them," charged the angry pitcher. "You could hold the runners on base. You almost cost us the game. I don't care whether you like me or not. But you ought to think enough of the team——"

"Who is talking?" broke in Dick, his eyes flashing and his fists clinched. "Who thinks more about the team than I do—unless it is Keith here? Who talked whose father into booking your brother so you could stay here through next week?"

Keith groaned. Dick and his temper!

Tom paled. "What are you talking about?" he demanded.

"Just what I said," Dick snapped. "Your brother was going to leave Austin and go back to where people fall for his corny style. We wanted you here to help us sew up the first half, so I asked my Dad to book Sonny Barton at the Club Caravan through next week. Isn't that so, Keith?"

All he could do was duck his head. How could he deny it? And he could not explain that none of this mattered anyhow, that the league directors would meet and more than likely decide Tom was ineligible for any more games.

"Is that true, Keith?"

Tom asked the question in a low odd voice.

"Yes," Keith admitted. "But I don't think it means— well, not quite how Dick put it——"

Words failed him. Nor was there any stopping the aroused Dick.

"My Dad expects his club to lose money next week," he went on mercilessly. "But he thinks it will get something back in free publicity. So who thinks what about which team?" He let out an ugly little laugh. "It looks to me like the Merrills think more of it than anybody else. Your brother will be the first 'git-tar' player to ever work the Club Caravan and probably the last."

Tom whirled around, leaping into the waiting taxi. His order sent the vehicle off in high gear.

Keith stared after it, his lips trembling.

"You shouldn't have said all of that," he finally managed to say.

Dick took a deep breath. "I guess not," he admitted ruefully. "But I just couldn't help it."

They walked a few steps in unhappy silence. "He won't work for the team," Dick muttered. "You know that as well as I do. He won't let Mr. Tracy teach him how to pace himself for a full game. That is why we started off in the cellar."

Keith nodded glumly.

They reached the intersection of Pecos Street and Bonnie Road. "I will see you tomorrow," Keith said tonelessly, turning right.

"Sure," Dick said weakly, continuing straight ahead.

The feelings between Tom and Dick did not mean anything to the team, Keith brooded. Not any more. Atlas would lose its pitching ace by vote of the directors anyhow. The Bartons would leave, too. Still, sighed Keith, he wished it had not happened. Now Tom would leave West Austin with a bad taste in his mouth. And he could not help the traits which had rubbed Dick and others the wrong way. Actually, Tom had done much about overcoming those faults. If he could spend an entire season under Mr. Tracy—Keith turned into his driveway. Why even think about that?

Especially after hearing the board's verdict from his father. The other directors had agreed with Mr. Gregg. This was carrying Little League enthusiasm entirely too far.

Tom Barton was ineligible by a unanimous vote.

CHAPTER 14

O

Mr. Merrill's Problem

There was no practice Friday. Keith watched from the stands as Calumet defeated Bedford 7–2. Now three teams were tied for second, third and fourth; the Giants proudly held first place with a full two game lead. The magic number was one, gloated Keith. One Atlas victory, or if the other teams split their next week's games, and the first half was won.

Keith meant to sleep later than usual that Saturday morning. But the visitor to the Gregg household arrived early and not at all quietly.

In fact, Mr. Merrill was very upset and did not bother to deny it.

"What do you mean the directors voted the boy ineligible?" His voice carried to Keith's bedroom. "Do you realize what your board has done to the Club Caravan? I tell you that Sonny Barton——" His voice lowered and Keith could not hear the rest of the protest.

He stole into the kitchen. His mother was at the drainboard preparing three cups of coffee.

"What is going on?" asked Keith, blinking sleep out of his eyes.

His mother turned to face him. Her eyes were twinkling and she seemed to be struggling to hold back a smile.

"I think it would be amusing if it was not so important to Mr. Merrill."

"What is it?" demanded Keith. Why must she talk in riddles?

"Sit down and I will tell you while I pour you a glass of milk. They can wait a minute for their coffee."

Keith obeyed.

"It is this booking next week at the Club Caravan," said his mother, now yielding to temptation and smiling. "You knew that Mr. Merrill did not expect Sonny Barton to appeal to the older people."

"Yes, ma'am," nodded Keith. "But he said something about free advertising——"

"Let me finish," said Mrs. Gregg. "You know that I like Sonny, so I cannot help enjoying it." Her smile came again. "Mr. Merrill and his club manager and his publicity man did not stop to think that Sonny has been singing only ballads and folk music on his television shows. And he has not worn his usual costumes before the cameras."

Keith nodded, getting impatient. Sure, he had noticed these things. He understood Sonny's motives, too—to get dates with Barbee Brush. "What of it?"

"Just this. The Club Caravan advertised Sonny Barton for a week and its telephones started ringing. Was he going to sing rock-and-roll or folk music and ballads as on his television program? If the latter, then——"

She stopped to laugh softly. "The club is near all reserved for next week, and here it is just Saturday morning."

"Gosh, that is good," mumbled Keith. "Then Mr. Merrill won't lose any money after all."

"It is *not* good," declared Mrs. Gregg, now serious. "For yesterday Sonny called the club and cancelled out. He told the assistant manager that he did not take bookings because of his younger brother's ability in Little League baseball. Mr. Purcell—he is the assistant manager—had no idea what Sonny was talking about. Mr. Merrill knew at once, of course. He tried to contact Sonny as soon as he learned about the cancellation. But they are gone, and they left no word where or how they could be contacted."

"You mean Sonny and Tom have left?"

"Exactly. Here Mr. Merrill is with a stack of reservations and no Sonny Barton. Telephone calls to Nashville and other places have told him nothing. Sonny is not in touch with his agent."

"But they can't—did they just pick up and leave——?"

"They just left," said Mrs. Gregg, "and Mr. Merrill is holding the bag. He has found out what Dick told Tom after the game Thursday and the directors' vote and—well, Mr. Merrill is not happy, I can tell you that."

At least Dick's father was quieter and calmer.

"I do not deny that I was approached in that spirit," he was saying to Mr. Gregg now, "and that Dick was justified in believing that was why we engaged Tom's brother. Dick is too young to understand about tax write-offs and publicity and such. I will not deny, either, that we were amazed by the public's response to young Barton. I had no idea that he had collected such a following with his new style of singing. Now what can we do about it?"

"I cannot suggest anything you have not already done," Mr. Gregg said. "Just keep trying. Sonny Barton and his brother cannot simply disappear into thin air, not in that car of his anyhow."

"He just *has* to come back for this week," brooded Mr. Merrill. "Maybe the following week, too. Gregg, the club never has had such response to a single attraction."

Keith, watching through the open door, saw Mr. Merrill rise suddenly and pace around his chair.

"And you say I cannot recover any damages?"

"You *cannot*," Mr. Gregg said immediately. "I am his attorney in Austin, until further notice, anyhow. You did not book him in any fair spirit. You expected him to fail as a drawing card and you meant to offset your loss in publicity at the expense of his professional dignity. He was quite justified in cancelling out."

"If Dick and Tom had not gotten into that squabble," sighed Mr. Merrill, "then Sonny would not have known——"

"But he did find out about your motive and he is gone. My advice is to redouble your efforts to find him, and then to throw yourself on his mercy."

Mrs. Gregg served their coffee, then rejoined Keith in the kitchen. "You are not amused either," she observed.

Keith shook his head. If Dick had just held—well, even so, the directors of the league would have voted the same way.

His mother patted his shoulder. "I know," she said

gently. "You are thinking more about Tom than his brother and the Club Caravan business. I don't blame you."

Keith sighed. "It is sort of a mess," he could not help saying.

"It certainly is," she conceded.

His eyes gleamed with sudden inspiration. "If Mr. Merrill finds Sonny, and he *will* come back for a week, then won't Tom be eligible to play with us?"

"I don't know what the directors would do in that case. But will they face that problem?"

"What do you mean?"

"Would Tom play if his brother did return for a week?" Mrs. Gregg's eyes clouded. "He has as much pride as Sonny, maybe even more so."

Keith could not deny that.

"But, first, Sonny must be located and——"

"Can't the police——?"

Keith shook his head. He knew the answer to his own question. No law was broken. Another sigh. So many "if's." *If* Dick had not lost his temper. *If* the Barton brothers had not left Austin so hurriedly. And, of course, *if* Atlas could win either of its two games next week!

Keith found Dave Parker and Abe Duran already in the dugout. No ball was available, so they held to the shade. Both knew of the sudden departure of the Barton brothers.

"It sure leaves us in the hole," Dave said unhappily. "You and Pat—who else can pitch?"

Keith nodded. Hadn't he worried about that for the past forty-eight hours? Miles Carowe had the makings of a pitcher but he would not be ready for this season.

"Well," sighed Abe, "Tom won us the first half, if we can beat either Bedford or Calumet next week."

Dick came into the dugout just then. "Tell our catcher that," Keith said, unable to keep a sour note out of his voice.

Abe repeated his statement. Dick just nodded.

"Sure. He *could* be the best pitcher this league ever had." His lips twitched and he looked at Keith appealingly. "I did not think he and his brother would leave town just because of what I said."

Keith sighed. That thought had not occurred to him either. Certainly he had not expected Sonny to cancel a week's booking and leave without a word to anyone. But, as his mother had pointed out, there was their fierce pride.

"Has your dad ever found Sonny?"

"He hadn't at noon. And, boy, is he upset!"

"I know," nodded Keith. "He came to see my father early today."

That had to be explained for the benefit of Dave and Abe.

"It doesn't make sense," shrugged the former. "I didn't care for his ballad singing either."

By then Mr. Tracy had arrived with the equipment. The other boys came up quickly; the fourteen of them sank down in the dugout while their manager sat on the concrete step.

"I can tell that you have heard about Tom," Mr. Tracy said evenly. "He did not just pick up and leave us. He was ineligible for any more games anyhow. The league directors voted him so and I could not oppose their action."

Quick questions came. Why was he ineligible? Mr. Tracy explained tersely and quickly, then cut off more talk.

He shifted his weight slightly. "That was a risk we took at the start of the season," he explained. "It paid off for us, too. We are in the driver's seat for this next half. It did not take too many points to get Tom. All managers realized that he would not be here all season.

"But we are going to miss him. We must develop another pitcher and an infielder in a hurry—by next Monday. Pat, you start throwing to batting practice. You hit first, Keith, then warm up with somebody. And, Miles, you get ready to throw, too."

Keith swung three bats as Pat took his warm-up pitches.

Mr. Dudley began hitting ground balls to Abe and Jac. Davis Gordon took their throws at first base.

Keith sighed. First, he had worked as a catcher, then as a first baseman. Now, he supposed, he could consider himself the Giant mound mainstay. For it was too much to expect a ten-year-old to develop into a full game pitcher. It would be next season anyhow before Pat would be strong enough to go the full route.

He could throw the ball; that was for sure. You only had to bat against him once to appreciate what Mr. Tracy described as a natural wrinkle. Pat's throws broke without any obvious effort on his part.

Keith fouled two behind him, then connected squarely. Even so, he managed only a fly which Tim Haley caught several steps from the fence. His next effort was a high hopper to Jac.

One more cut. Keith waited for a letter high pitch and swung with all his force. He "got a piece" of the ball and that was all. Roy easily caught the short fly in center.

Keith shook his head ruefully and surrendered the plate

to Joe Pettus. Selecting a ball, he engaged José Aguirre to catch for him.

Toeing the practice rubber outside the right field foul line, he was facing Enfield Road. And so he was the first to see the yellow convertible turn into the gate. There was the driver and a smaller edition of him on the front seat—Tom.

Others noticed the car almost as soon as Keith. And recognized it instantly, too. Who could fail to do that?

Sonny Barton!

The flashy automobile stopped behind the left field set of bleachers. Out scrambled Tom with a wide grin of greeting for Keith and José. He had his glove, noticed Keith, as if intending to practice.

Keith saw that Mr. Tracy had come to the gate and waited there. Sonny was out of the car now.

"Ah am sorry Tom is late, Mr. Tracy," Keith heard the singer say apologetically. "It is mah fault. Ah drove as fast as ah dared, but we just got back in town."

Keith stopped throwing, pretending thirst. But he was more interested in what was being said than in the water fountain.

"Haven't you heard what the league directors voted about Tom, Sonny?"

"No, sir."

"They ruled Tom ineligible, by a unanimous vote."

A puzzled scowl formed on the famous olive-colored features.

"Why should they do that, Mr. Tracy?"

"Because of your next week's booking at the Club Caravan. That was proposed to Mr. Merrill just so Tom could play out the first half with us."

"Ah know that, suh," Sonny said slowly. "My brother told me. So ah am not singing there. But what does that have to do with Tom?'

"Didn't you and Tom leave town? I understood that Mr. Merrill has been unable to reach you."

Sonny showed a faint smile. "We started, Mr. Tracy. Ah admit that. We got as far as Palestine, going back to Tennessee. Then ah decided to do something else that sure suits Tom. Ah turned around and we came back to Austin as fast as we could. And here we stay."

Now, realized the excited team, it was Mr. Tracy's turn to be puzzled.

"What do you mean, Sonny?"

"Ah mean ah am going to quit singing and finish high school and then go to college. Right here in Austin."

"You are *retiring* and locating here, permanently?"

"Yes, suh. This is our home and for sure," Sonny said firmly. "Tom and ah both want it that way. We like it here." A smile again. "Ah have no idea where ah stand in school. Ah may have to start in behind my kid brother."

Never before had Keith seen Mr. Tracy at a loss for words. But the manager was now.

"Sonny," he asked finally, "can you just *quit*?"

"Ah have done it," shrugged the singer. His dark eyes twinkled. "Oh, ah made enough money already, Mr. Tracy. And ah will have royalties coming in from records—for a long time, ah hope. Tom and ah will get along all right."

"I am sure you will, Sonny," Mr. Tracy said. "I am sure you will," he repeated. He turned to Tom.

"All right, partner. Take a couple of fast laps, then fall in somewhere and take your turn at bat."

The boy darted off. But Sonny Barton was not finished.

"Another thing, Mr. Tracy," he said quietly. "Tom and ah talked quite a bit on the way back. Ah think you will find him easier to handle from now on."

"If he is," said the manager, his eyes twinkling, "then he will be quite a pitcher by the end of the season."

Sonny returned to his car. Mr. Tracy started back through the gate. Keith could control himself no longer. He caught the manager's elbow.

"The directors—they will vote again, won't they?" he asked breathlessly. "They will change their ruling about Tom."

"I don't see how they can do otherwise," Mr. Tracy said with a chuckle. "This changes the picture entirely."

He gestured toward Sonny. Now the singer was moving to take a seat in the first base bleachers.

"Did you notice, Keith?" Mr. Tracy asked gently. "Blue jeans and plain shirt."

Keith stared. It was true. He had just paid no attention. Tom Barton was wearing worn trousers and shirt instead of his usual regalia.

"Now if he would just get his hair cut," Keith thought aloud.

"I believe," mused Mr. Tracy, "I will insist on that. And before Monday's game, too. After all, a manager should have some rights."

Mr. Gregg arrived before the end of practice. Shortly Mr. Thomas came, too. They talked to Sonny for long minutes away from the other spectators, then sat with the singer in the bleachers.

The president and the players' agent—what they believed would influence the other directors. It was all Keith could do to concentrate on practice. He ran to his father the instant Mr. Tracy dismissed them.

"Dad, did you know——!"

"Yes, yes," Mr. Gregg broke in. "We all know about it. Sonny Barton has given up his career and his younger brother is as much a resident of this area as you are."

"Then the directors will meet again and——?"

"There is nothing to meet about, Keith," said Mr. Thomas, a smile playing over his ruddy features. "Tom meets every requirement of the league. Your father has ruled so and I have upheld him."

"Yippee!" whooped Keith. Now he dared to believe it. He ran to Tom, starting to climb into the car with his brother. "You are going to be here all season!"

"Sure," grinned Tom. He pounded his glove. "And Babe Ruth League next year," he said happily. "Then American Legion and on through high school."

"Get in, Keith," offered Sonny. "Ah will take you home."

Keith hesitated. What about Dick? They walked home together after every practice and game. Dick often refused rides to go with Keith.

"You had better get in," said Sonny. "Ah am trading off this fancy job next week."

"Trading your car?"

"Sure," Sonny said lightly. "This is no car for a schoolboy. Ah will get something smaller and not so flashy. Maybe ah will get a jeep station wagon."

Keith still hesitated. Tom seemed to sense his worry.

"Wait, Sonny," he asked. Then he called out to Dick Merrill, starting toward the opposite gate.

"Dick? Come ride with us."

The catcher turned. His eyes went from Tom to Keith, then back again.

"Sure," he said a bit gruffly. "Sure," he said again, moving to join Tom in the back seat.

They were blocked at the gate by Mr. Merrill. A relieved Mr. Merrill, too—that was plain to see.

"Boy, am I glad to see you!" exclaimed Dick's father, coming out of his car quickly. "We have tried everywhere to locate you."

"Yes, suh," Sonny said quietly. "Mr. Gregg told me about it. Ah am sorry to be so much trouble."

He paused, drumming lightly on his steering wheel. "Ah had already decided to quit, Mr. Merrill," he said slowly. "But Mr. Gregg thinks ah ought to fill this last booking. And ah sure don't want to leave on a sour note."

He changed positions under the wheel. "You thought you would lose money on me, Mr. Merrill," he went on. "Ah don't believe so." His dark eyes glistened. "You advertise that it is Sonny Barton's last professional stand, you will get some customers."

"We can advertise that?"

"Yes, suh."

Mr. Merrill's eyes dropped. He studied the ground a minute, then looked up. "We don't deserve that, Sonny," he said, his voice sort of strained. "I don't. The club doesn't."

"You got it," smiled the older Barton.

"Then we will do our best with it," promised Mr. Merrill. He hesitated. "They will want you to sing ballads and folk music, too, Sonny."

The singer's swarthy features held their smile. "Whatever the folks want, Mr. Merrill. But mostly rock-and-roll the last night, suh. That is how ah came in, and that is the way ah am going out."

CHAPTER 15

O

Turn Around, Turn Around

"Think of it," said Mr. Gregg with a sigh. "Retiring already—at his age. And with not only a living for himself the rest of his life, but a start for his brother."

"What does he intend to make of himself?"

"That is the ironic part," said Mr. Gregg. "He wants to be a lawyer. Can you imagine?"

Keith looked up from his homework. He had startled his parents by starting on an English assignment which was not due until Monday. Usually he never thought of lessons until Sunday night.

"What is wrong with that?"

"I have a case in court next week," his father said dryly. "But I don't expect over a thousand people to pay a cover charge to see me perform. Nor am I able to retire after only a few years in the profession."

He took a sip of his coffee. "By the way," he said to his wife, an almost sheepish expression coming to his features,

"I made reservations for Saturday night. We have not been to a supper club in a long time."

"Too long," agreed Mrs. Gregg.

"You mean you are going to pay to hear him sing?" demanded Keith. "I thought you didn't like him."

"You will understand some day," his mother said. "Now work on your theme. And let me go over it before you hand it in."

"Yes, ma'am."

Keith obeyed. But it still made no sense, he mused. He finished his paper and turned it over to Mrs. Gregg for her inspection. She made a correction or two, then returned it to be recopied. With that Keith went to bed, but not immediately to sleep.

Bedford tomorrow, Calumet Thursday! Win either game and the first half belonged to the Giants. And with Tom Barton for the rest of the season—especially one willing to be taught how to pace himself. Keith scowled at the moonlight streaming in through the window. He should be learning that himself, perhaps. For there was no reason not to consider a pitching future for himself even if catching was still his favorite position.

Could they beat the Dodgers? Sure, he chortled. He just hoped that Tom did not wear himself out and Mr. Tracy would not change pitchers. Then, Keith schemed, if he could build himself up to a full game hurler—how they would be fixed for the second half. Tom and himself as starters, Pat in relief!

Keith saw the two figures from a block away and wondered who could be already practicing. Nearing the field, he recognized Tom and Sonny. The former had a new fungo and was hitting line drives to his brother. Sonny, in wet shapeless T-shirt and stained blue jeans, was chasing the hits as hard as if trying out for Little League himself.

Dick and Jac reached the field on Keith's heels. Sonny came to the dugout, perspiration streaming down his face and neck. More Giants arrived, then Mr. Tracy and the equipment. Sonny left the field for the bleachers.

"Now remember," Keith overheard him say to his brother, "you pitch to signals. No more showing off."

The entire team was in the dugout by ten minutes to four. Keith beamed proudly. Nobody could charge this squad with lack of eagerness.

Mr. Tracy took his usual place, on the concrete step.

"You know what we have to do," he said tersely. "It sounds easy—just win one game. But we will face their best pitchers, remember that. You will hit against Rene today, then Chastain Thursday. If we lose both games, and finish in a tie, we will have a one-game playoff Saturday. The six-inning limit will hold on all pitchers. So will the seventy-two hour rule. Our pitching staff is not that deep. If we are forced into a playoff, we will lose."

His gray eyes swept their faces. "We almost lost to Winston Friday. Remember? We eked out by inches. Seth Mitchell almost caught Dick's fly. Pat's bunt hit a clump of grass and rolled dead. That was how we scored three runs. We were lucky. We had better not depend on breaks this week."

Mr. Dudley vaulted over the fence in time to throw batting practice.

"Get set for curves," warned the assistant manager. "I am not throwing any straight balls."

And he kept his promise. Keith swung five times against Mr. Dudley's version of a roundhouse. One was hit solidly, the rest were pop-ups or easy rollers.

But this should better prepare them to face Rene's wide assortment of pitches.

Tom fared better than most of his teammates. A curve did not seem to bother him. He just met it squarely, making no effort to clout the ball.

"Hit like that in games," said Mr. Tracy, "and you would really help us."

"Yes, sir," Tom nodded. "I will."

Off he went to warm up. It took him a long time to get ready, thought Keith, which hurt his chances to hurl a full game. Pat, now, could throw five balls and be "warm." So could Keith.

Tom came back to the dugout wearing a new blue warm-up jacket.

"I sure would like to go six innings, Mr. Tracy," he said, almost timidly. "I believe I know what you mean by pacing myself, and I am sure I can do it."

"You can if you concentrate, Tom," agreed Mr. Tracy. "But let's not decide about six innings now. If you go more than three, you cannot pitch at all Thursday. Maybe we will want to take that chance and maybe not."

The Dodgers took the field. There was no doubt of their spirit, decided Keith.

Then out went the Giants from the third base dugout. We were never better, Keith gloated after a minute. Dick was throwing hard and straight to second base. Abe seemed to be covering more ground at third.

We are ready, Keith whispered.

And Jac proved it immediately. He led off with a single between short and third.

Tom stepped into the box. Applause came from both sides of the field. The story was well-known by now, of course; the Barton brothers were permanent residents of West Austin. Keith smiled. Tom did not appear to notice the demonstration. He was intent on Rene's right arm.

Keith was expecting a sacrifice, as was the Dodger infield, which came in close. But the combination of Mr. Tracy and the batting practice came up with a surprising play. Joe broke for second just as Tom swung. The Giant pitcher poked a grounder between first and second.

Billy Harper, moving with Jac, could not recover in time. He trapped the ball but both runners were safe.

Now Joe Pettus. He let two pitches pass for a one-one count, then did the expected. His bunt toward first easily advanced both runners.

"Meet it, Dave," Keith said to Parker.

The outfielder nodded and carefully set his feet forward in the box, choking his bat slightly. Usually Dave took a big cut. Now he seemed determined to just hit the ball center.

He swung at Rene's second offering and lifted a fly into right center. Bedford's Bart French caught the sinking ball with a desperate lunge. He fell forward with the effort and so had no chance to stop Jac from scoring, or Joe from taking third.

Keith now, also standing well up, determined not to overswing. He was pitched tight by the grim Rene and he hit off the handle. Shortstop McMillan easily caught the blooper.

The difference in Tom's pitching showed against the first

batter. He threw the first one squarely over. Manager Collins of the Dodgers was well-known for having his hitters take the initial pitch. Keith remembered the manager's explanation. It allowed a boy to "settle" in the box and time the pitcher's speed.

But it also gave the hurler a big strike, if he came right across with the ball. And, leading 1–0, sure of himself, Tom baited the batter with a pitch slightly high and outside. Bill Harper "fished," as many batters would.

The strikeout was set up now. A sweeping curve would probably send Billy back to the dugout. But Mr. Tracy had cautioned Tom against trying to fan batters.

"You are leading the league in strikeouts," the manager had pointed out, "but you have never pitched and won a complete game. Those are the statistics which count."

It was a letup, a change of pace which caught Harper flat-footed. He neither swung nor looked back to ask the umpire's decision.

Dick whipped the ball to Keith and on around the horn it went, then back to the pitcher.

Another first strike called. Keith called approval to Tom and pounded his mitt. Was Tom calm and deliberate enough to suit Mr. Tracy? If not, then it was impossible to satisfy the manager. For this slim pitcher seemed no more concerned than if throwing batting practice.

A curve to Dewey Held, but nothing like Tom's best effort. Dewey slashed a grounder to Jac. The pint-sized shortstop fielded it cleanly and threw carefully to Keith.

Two gone. Tom McMillan up for Bedford.

"Two away, Tom," Mr. Tracy called to his pitcher.

Keith understood the manager's reason for this warning.

Mr. Tracy claimed defensive teams often "let down" unintentionally after two outs. More games were won with two out than in any other circumstances, he said. Two out— that was the time to bear down, not ease up.

Tom nodded. He fingered the resin bag, then grimly faced McMillan. The first pitch blazed across the plate. The second, a curve, broke wide but still drew the batter's swing. Dick stabbed desperately at the throw but it eluded him.

"No harm done," Keith told the pitcher.

Tom nodded again. This third offering was shoulder high and inside. McMillan swung weakly as he pulled back.

The weak roller was right to Abe Duran. It should have been an easy out, but suddenly Abe was all thumbs. McMillan was already at the base before the third baseman could get ready to throw.

"Nobody hurt," Keith called anxiously, walking the ball back to the mound.

Another nod. Usually these silly sort of errors upset Tom. His reaction to them before had been to set his lips and decide to get the opposition out by his own efforts. Could Tom stay calm with a runner on first and Marty Kuhlman at the plate?

Then McMillan was on second, the count one and one. Dick had failed to block a breaking curve.

Marty was a powerful hitter—not too consistent, but apt to clear the bases any time he swung. Tom dealt up another curve. Marty missed. Keith groaned as Dick slapped the ball down, then threw too late to catch McMillan at third.

"One more, big Tom," chattered Keith. Thank goodness

there were two outs and batters could get first base because of a missed third strike. Forget the runner, just get the ball past Kuhlman.

And Tom did. His curve dipped away from both the flailing bat and Dick's groping mitt. The ball even thudded against the backstop. But who cared? The Dodgers were out in their half of the first.

And Tom Barton did not seem too upset by Dick's ineptness behind the plate.

"I just can't hold that curve when you bear down," Dick confessed ruefully. "But throw it anyhow. I'll find some way to stop them."

"We got them out," said Tom with a shrug. "That is all that counts."

More runs—Keith yelled that to his teammates as he took the first base coaching position. But Davis, Joe, and Dick went out in quick succession. They hit Rene and fairly solidly, but the Dodgers gave their pitching stout backing.

Tom bore down against Larry Cripps, fanning the opposing first baseman. Now Bedford's heavy hitters were out of the way. Rene lined to Joe. Bart French singled through the box. An error let Jim Burns take first and Bart second.

That two out situation again, groaned Keith.

"Fire it in, Tom boy," he called out.

It would not do to let Mutt Camp fill the bases and bring up the top of Bedford's batting order.

Keith watched the pitcher anxiously. Tom must be discouraged. What pitcher could help it? He was trying to pace himself as per his manager's instructions but his shaky defense forced him to seize the load single-handed.

He went to the resin bag, then toed the rubber with some of his old fierceness. Three blazing strikes set down the Dodger right fielder.

Keith sighed as Pat and Tom went to the bullpen. Tom was being made to throw too many pitches, no doubt of it. And it made little difference as to the cause. The important thing was not to lose this game in the late innings because of a tiring starter.

More runs would help, of course.

Jac singled with one out but Billy Harper made a fine catch of Tom's line drive. And Rene himself stabbed Joe's solid smash.

One-nothing still. It seemed to Keith that Tom showed tenseness on the mound.

"Just get it over," the first sacker said cheerfully. "We have all the errors out of our systems now."

This was *the* inning as far as going the route was concerned. Mr. Tracy—if he had not decided already—must determine his strategy between now and the start of the fourth.

"Let's rise and shine," Keith yelled to his teammates. "It's time for us to help the pitcher a little."

The Giant infield rallied to this cry. Jac scooped up a bounder over second and made a fine throw. Abe went to the fence for Dewey's foul. Two gone. McMillan was up, but with no runners on base. Still, with the Dodger shortstop adept at getting up and the strong Kuhlman on deck—Keith was not surprised that Tom Barton bore down with his "Sunday" pitches. Twice Dick had to go to the backstop for throws which got away from him. But McMillan had swung at both, and had missed, and now the Bedford shortstop was fooled by an easy curve. He lifted a weak effort to Tom for the third out.

Dave Parker's home run made it 2–0. Keith saw Mr. Tracy hesitate as Joe Weiman fanned for the third out. It was no easy choice; Keith was happy that he did not have to make it himself. If Tom weakened, as he had early in the season, and the Dodgers pulled this game out——!

The tall manager gestured for Tom to continue on the mound. Keith felt like whooping with joy. If Tom could continue in control of himself, the Giants would sew up the first half this game.

But there was no easing up with Kuhlman, Cripps, and Rene due up.

"Nothing good, boy," Keith called to Tom.

The slim pitcher had no intention of grooving one for Kuhlman. But neither did Tom cut loose with his fierce curves. He pitched the Dodger catcher carefully, keeping the ball on the outside corner.

It was the first time Keith had seen the younger Barton depend on control against a strong hitter. Kuhlman, standing well away from the plate, did not like outside and low offerings. He let the first go for a strike. A ball. A third one in the same spot. A second called strike.

Keith saw Tom take a deep breath. Nobody could blame the hurler if he tried for a strikeout now. But he threw to Marty's weakness again, perhaps a bit more outside.

Marty felt he had to swing. He punched a roller which bounded into Keith's mitt. An easy out, of course.

Larry Cripps. Mr. Tracy signaled from the dugout for Tom to play this batter the same way, low and outside.

The first offering touched the outside corner for a called strike. Keith chortled. How was this for calmness and self-confidence in a hurler? *Letting* Kuhlman and Cripps hit, just working the corners!

Larry slashed the next pitch hard. It streaked over Abe at third and seemed headed for extra bases. But a left-handed batter hitting late—the ball's curve carried it foul by no more than a step.

Larry had almost reached first, preparing to turn for a bid at second. Back to the plate he went with a disgusted look.

"Just a long strike, Tom boy," Keith called.

But he could not help feeling concerned. He knew how those solidly smashed fouls bothered a pitcher.

Larry was hugging the plate, bat choked, ready to hit anything on the outside corner. Tom turned to his curve. It broke sharply, driving Larry out of the box. Inside for a ball.

"Good pitch," Keith called.

So it had been. If Cripps crowded again——

There he crouched. Tom shook off the first signal. He threw his curve again. It was on the inside corner if not out of the strike zone. But Larry punched at it anyhow. He hit a high hopper right back to the mound.

Keith saw Tom sigh, as if in relief. Was the pitcher tiring? He threw to Rene as if lacking his usual speed. But the opposing hurler went out, too, lining to Joe.

Keith ran to Tom. "Are you all right?"

"Sure," the hurler said lightly. "I just threw two balls hard."

The fifth should be an easy inning for him, worried Keith. Coming up for Bedford—French, Burns, and Camp.

If Tom could coast by this trio, then he could go all out in the sixth. Or, if the Giants could manage more runs——

Not in that frame. In the fifth, yes—after three Dodgers went out in order, all hitting fair balls, two to the Giant outfield.

Then Atlas came up with two more runs. Four–nothing now, gloated Keith . Just three outs to go.

"How do you feel, Tom?" asked Mr. Tracy.

"Like I haven't pitched," said the slim boy with a shrug. "I have had it easy today, Mr. Tracy."

"You have made it easy," the manager said. He hesitated. "Three to go. If you aren't tired—pitch us in."

"You mean—bear down?"

"Strike them out and let's go home," the manager said tersely.

Keith saw Tom's lips twitch. He walked to the mound and threw his warm-ups quickly. He toed the rubber and waited for Bill Harper to step into the box.

Tom was tense now, his lips set, a gleam in his eyes. And his expression—Keith kicked up dirt as he shifted to play tight against Harper. Where had he seen that look before? He remembered suddenly. Sonny Barton had showed that same expression on the night of the Cub Scout benefit. So he had faced the audience which had roared with laughter at the burlesque of his rock-and-roll style. His voice had not showed any defiance. He had explained gently that he would sing a lullaby taught him by his mother. But his expression—Keith could see it plainly now. Sort of like daring someone to do something—defiance that was the word. Pride, too, and self-confidence. Could one look express all three things at the same time?

And how had that song gone? Turn around, that was it.

Turn around, turn around, and you are a wee one. So the Barton brothers had first faced West Austin, with a surprising change of pace. What people had expected—Sonny was not that at all. Nor his younger brother this day. Four–nothing. He had thrown every pitch exactly according to Mr. Tracy's pattern. Even now—Mr. Tracy's orders—pitch us in, Tom.

Two fast balls for called strikes, then a curve dipping low. Dick fell in front of it. The ball bounded off his chest protector and against the barricade protecting the Atlas dugout. But who cared. One out! Keith took Dick's delayed throw and flipped to Joe. Around the horn, back to the pitcher waiting with that same set, grim expression.

Tiring? Here it was the sixth and Tom Barton had more stuff than at any other time in the game.

Strike one.

That fierce look on his swarthy face—Keith chortled. You just had to look at Tom Barton to know this game was in the bag. Turn around, Keith hummed to himself. Turn around, turn around, for we are the champions, the champions of this long first half. Turn around, turn around, and we are the champions, and there is just one half to go.

Strike two.

Keith could not help chuckling at Dick's expression. The catcher was rubbing his right thigh with a scowl. The curve had missed his mitt and smashed into his unprotected flesh.

Was he all right? Keith saw Tom's lips frame the question. Dick motioned the pitcher back to the mound.

Strike three!

Dick slapped this down bare-handed. He took his time

picking up the ball and flipping it to Keith. He took the final throw of the horn and handed the ball to Tom.

"Just one to go," he gloated.

"Sure," the pitcher whispered.

All at once he seemed to have lost his fierceness. He studied both batter and catcher with a faraway look. His eyes moved to the third base section of the stands. There Sonny sat.

The slim pitcher stepped off the rubber and touched the resin bag. His dark eyes circled his teammates, then back to his catcher. No sign of tenseness now, observed Keith. And the smile on the hurler's features—gentle, easy. Almost shy.

He shook off two signals. Then he tossed over his letup.

The Dodger shortstop was braced for speed or a curve, not this tantalizing pitch. He tried to hold up but his bat came around anyhow. He sent a slower roller to Jac.

The shortstop charged, took the ball bare-handed, threw without raising up.

He *had* to hurry; McMillan could travel down the baseline. The throw was high and inside. Keith leaped and snared it one-handed. He flung out his mitt desperately, for he had been pulled off the bag. His pad brushed something and Keith knew he had touched the runner.

Out. Keith ran to embrace the slim, swarthy pitcher. Other Giants charged to the mound, too, including those out of the dugout.

Turn around, chortled Keith, turn around.

About the Author

In his early teens Curtis Bishop began writing sports stories for a daily newspaper. At the University of Texas he twice edited *The Texas Ranger*, the college magazine. His athletic interests included all sports—with emphasis on tennis, in which he was a sectional champion, and semi-pro baseball. He divided his time among working in the oil fields, announcing championship rodeos, and newspaper work until World War II, when he joined the Foreign Broadcast Intelligence Service and saw duty in two theaters of war. Mr. Bishop's first book was published in 1947. Since then, he has had some forty-five books published.

In 1953 Curtis Bishop became interested in baseball for youngsters and organized a team in his native Austin which included his oldest son, Barry. The team racked up three championships in as many years. Another son, Burk, carried on the family tradition by playing on two championship clubs and joined his brother in winning all-star honors. Mr. Bishop has since continued his active role in Little League baseball.